FRANCES JOHNSON

Frances Johnson

STACEY LEVINE

VERSE CHORUS PRESS

Published by Verse Chorus Press
PO Box 14806, Portland OR 97293. www.versechorus.com

First published in 2005 by Clear Cut Press.

The author would especially like to thank Corrina Wycoff, Glenn MacGilvra, Matthew Stadler, Emily White, Rich Jensen, Deborah Woodard, Paul Constant, the Levines, and Steve Connell at Verse Chorus Press.

Copyedited by Allison Dubinsky
Book design by Transgraphic (www.transgraphic.net)
Cover image enhancement by Scott Nasburg

A portion of this book appeared in the *Santa Monica Review*.

4 CULTURE This book was written with assistance from the 4Culture Commission of King County, Washington.

ISBN 978-1-891241-29-1

Library of Congress Control Number: 2010925517

for CEMW

Frances Johnson sat on her front porch, listening to the radio in the dark. She wore a blue dress.

Beyond the wooden porch, night was thick. Frances stood, walking into the living-room, listening. A train lumbered across a nearby trestle, halting as it reached the center of the weak bridge. Below the trestle was a curving road, leading in one direction toward the town, and in the opposite direction toward the sea.

The train hissed. It would follow a tricky, meandering route that would probably lead to another state.

Frances was an expressive woman in many ways.

There were so many people and things to think about, such huge compendiums of circumstances.

Sometimes Frances was afraid for no real reason, it seemed. Oftentimes, waking in the middle of the night, she was uncertain who she was. Frances did not like that. Stumbling to the bathroom, she feared that who or whatever she was would be inappropriate or cause a calamity of some kind—and that was the most frightening thing of all. Standing on a little foot-rug, she would calm herself by rubbing her limbs briskly, hoping the heat would fill out her body and make it more dimensional.

"We can't know the future," she said dully to some-one on the telephone, then hung up the heavy receiver.

Outside, the porch swing creaked.

"I will not attend the dance," she spoke aloud to herself.

Frances had a suitor, Ray Garn. Ray was fine, though sometimes his enthusiasms were hard to understand. The two had been together for quite some time, making vague, halfhearted plans for the future.

Ray was mild-tempered, and things generally went well. Once, though, they traveled a few miles south to search for the sea — just that once — and Ray hid behind a wall for hours, causing Frances to feel a kind of fury.

It was a long, tall wall that rose up to hide the ocean shore from the road. Ray squatted next to it, smoking, smiling, and looking up at Frances when she found him, as if it were all a game, as if he had made her worry on purpose by hiding. She got so angry that she smacked him, hard, on the jaw.

He laughed. "Frances, it was just a joke! You know — hide-and-seek? Well, now you can hide, if you like."

Frances did not want to. She preferred to go into the cabin and play a quiet game by herself with a bowl of salty water, a religious-type game in which she imagined punishing and bathing herself and others. Sitting alone, in any case, brought such relief that Frances locked Ray out for most of the trip, feeling deliciously private while he stood by the sea with its freezing waves.

After some time, she saw through the cabin window that Ray had resorted to taking a walk. The wall along the beach prevented him from looking at the sea — assuming he liked the sea—and clamorous, gusty winds ripped at his sleeves and hair.

Frances left the cabin to join him at the far end of the wall. They said nothing at first, but soon were sharing some hard crackers and butter, sitting in the wild grass near the fence, chatting amicably and joking, shouting into the wind.

That evening she allowed Ray into the cabin bedroom, which smelled cheerlessly of mothballs and skin. He lay next to her on the bed for a while, then, levering upon bent arms, rolled atop her. She heard a tiny click: Ray's eyes shifting. After moments, he rolled away.

"It doesn't make sense to me," she exhaled toward the window, which framed a dark, gelatinous sky. "Two adults, in the middle of the night . . . one lying on top of the other . . . ?" Frances felt out of sorts.

"Yes, it's awfully strange," Ray agreed.

They fell asleep.

After the vacation, the pair got along fine. There was no reason to argue, they said, and each day vanished quickly, as if eager to flee the world. While not exactly gloomy, Frances regarded Ray with some sense of puzzlement.

Frances could not perceive Ray easily. She noticed, when physically close to him, that his head loomed so near and large she lost the sense of what he really looked like or who he was altogether; she would wonder why she was positioned next to him at all. She did not always enjoy their time together. But Frances stuck with Ray, on some days forgetting about him entirely. Her parents did not care for him, which was disappointing, but on the other hand, he was dependable, and good at bicycle tire repair.

It seemed she loved Ray.

Whom did Frances Johnson love?

Tonight, she looked at the door.

Ray was there. He looked down over his broad, tanned face.

"If things keep going the way they are, well, I think someday soon there might be a revolt!"

He was referring to their town, Munson. Years before, it had been called Hutchinson-Munson, after the pair of entrepreneur brothers-in-law who had founded the city upon a dream of a prosperous smelter. That business failed for countless reasons, the unpredictable Florida weather being only one of these. Still, the brothers-in-law strove to become famous, because they feared sudden death and the nothingness that might come after. So they became joint mayor of the town, writing a pamphlet about the local volcano and its stolid beauty before fleeing the region. Now, the town was simply known as Munson.

Munson was isolated, though at its border stood a sister town, Little-Munson, which was poor and weak. The people there always seemed to struggle for the simplest things.

Ray often expressed irritation with Munson, because, as he put it, the town preferred to forget—perhaps hide from—the outer world. Others, including Frances, were inclined to feel the same. Certainly there were worse places to live, towns that lacked even a council. But Munson had a strange air; besides, it had too many rules.

"Oh, Ray, who's going to revolt? There's no one to revolt," she said tiredly, glancing at his dark sweater-vest. Frances did not care about Ray's childhood or his life before they were together. She did not bother to inquire about his former girlfriends, though sometimes she saw Ray gazing at a wallet photograph of a girl sitting on the lap of a tough-looking older man: the girl's father, who had been prominent in a long-ago war. The girl was Fluff Davis, with whom Ray had spent a year or so. He doted on the old picture, even kissed it once, Frances observed, perhaps in admiration for the soldier father.

He opened the door. "Hmm," Ray began. "There've been plenty of revolts through history—peasants revolted during the reformation in Germany. Ha! They thought Martin Luther was on their side."

"Please, can't you take that discussion to your friends or brother?" Frances grew tired of Ray's overly detailed references to battle. "Give me some advice. I need something for this problem of mine." She shut her eyes and lay back on the beige sofa.

"What is it, Frances?" He sat nearby.

"Oh, the not-sleeping, I guess."

"Yes. It's awful for you! What can we do?"

"All those pots and pots of coffee to wake me up! I feel sick, thinking of it. And the sleeping pills to get me down at night—I don't necessarily like taking them, you know."

"I know. Well, can't we—"

"My heart could even burst! Could it?"

"Oh, no, Frances, no—that doesn't happen."

"Look at my eyes—these eyes are tired. I can barely get up in the morning."

"Frances, let Palmer help. I'll call him and make an appointment for you."

Frances scowled. She said, "Can't you just stay here, Ray? Let me lie in bed, with you on one side, and the telephone on the other, just for the night! Please."

Ray laughed. "Ho, I suppose that might be all right."

"Thanks! And Ray, don't talk about Napoleon, all right?"

"All right." Ray undressed. He was plump, and that pleased Frances. She looked away, thinking of other things: the insomnia, the strange non sequiturs she overheard neighbors speaking through the phone lines, and her dog. Immediately, she fell into a hapless, jagged doze, only to wake moments later, frightened back from the horizon of unconsciousness, for she had seen a turtle there.

Munson was hard on folks, she guessed, tossing in the bed, punching back the stiff coverlet. There was a sense of shame and difficulty in the town, though it was hard to say why. It wasn't easy to find another point of view, either, since Munson didn't much care for newcomers, and they stayed away. Companies and industries—ones that made gadgets—rarely settled in Munson or the adjoining Little-Munson, though they headed in sure droves for other Florida towns.

Frances recalled passing along Munson's main street that day and seeing the remains of a tattered, blowing poster on a pole asking as to the whereabouts of Josh White. He had been, she recalled, an argumentative boy of about thirteen. A year ago, Josh White had gone looking for his dog, who had run into Munson's oil-black nighttime streets. It seemed that the dog was lost, but it had in fact been detained by one of the town's sheriffs, and later the dog died, though no one could say why, only that there had been some type of a mix-up. Josh White got mad then. He fought loudly with his mother all that week in their cabin on the forest hill. The boy told his mother he would never forget the dog, though she pleaded with him to do so. But over the next month Josh White grew worse, not better, walking alone through the town late at night, hurling dirt chunks at Hodgkins' Movie House and other local businesses. Finally, his state of mind seemed to turn entirely: when spoken to, the boy would only open a wet, rosy mouth to scream, so in a short while, his mother took him to Ohio. After weeks the boy returned, again milling around town resentfully, and shortly after that, no one ever saw Josh White again. Secretly, Frances was a bit envious of the teenager, if only because she wanted to leave Munson, too.

Lately, Frances had been thinking of various plans to leave, but they seemed to her shaky, laughable plans.

Ray pulled back the bedclothes, and Frances' nose whistled with air. The atmosphere in the bedroom was one of contained quiet, as if the little room itself were keenly balanced on a pole. And at the other end of the pole, creating the balance—what was that? Maybe all the pills and pots of coffee, Frances considered wryly, turning over, eyes open.

She looked up. Everything seemed all right.

"Asleep?" Ray said.

She made no answer, and soon heard a muted clicking: the sound of Ray picking at his front tooth. She dozed.

In the late morning, Frances and Ray dressed together and unrolled their town paper. The sun was bright and high. Frances had awoken rather easily, with less exhaustion than usual, and in a burst of energy, she giggled at something Ray said.

Then, there came the sound of a blast. The house vibrated. Another booming noise seemed to burst hollowly into the first, causing both Frances and Ray to yell reflexively as the bedroom window shook. In the backyard, a small wooden fence toppled over.

She raised her eyes to the ceiling. Yes, it had happened again! A volcano was situated in the sea outside Munson, though Frances so often forgot. Sometimes it rumbled like this. The vibration manipulated the ground such that it trembled; this was at times followed by fierce winds, fires, an d even steam puffs dotting the sky. Townsfolk occasionally referred to the volcano as "Sharla," but just as often, they didn't think about it at all.

The house rattled with a moaning wind, and, in spite of herself, Frances was frightened, her heart beating hard enough that she felt her pulse in her eyes. She looked around the room: but where to go? "This is awful!" she cried, diving onto the bed next to Ray.

"It'll probably be fine!" he shouted reassuringly.

They lay still. The sounds of rushing wind and debris continued; briefly, the sky dimmed. A few fist-sized chunks of rough rock tumbled across the roof onto Frances' lawn. It's as if another world has come crashing into this one, she thought.

Ray clutched a tissue. "That damned volcano!"

"Let's just wait," she said.

They did.

Soon, light eased into the room again. The pair relaxed, then fell asleep; after waking, Frances felt better for the extra rest.

"Ray," she muttered dreamily then, looking to his glossy eyes. "I don't think I've ever asked you directly. How old are you?"

"Thirty-six. And you?"

"Thirty-eight. We're the same age, really."

They smiled together.

When Ray stood, he remarked, "Why, you look as helpless as a little girl, all wrapped in that blanket!" Then he moved to the bathroom.

Frances reached for the whisk broom and dustpan in her bedside table and began to sweep, eyeing the black telephone, a hot, serpentine anger climbing at the back of her throat because of Ray's remark. At times he was maddeningly superior, she felt, in a way that made her want to shout.

She looked through the living-room window, facing the yellowish light, glimpsing outside the refuse blown by the eruption and what appeared to be a large dog lying in the street. She turned away, shivering. All the nice things about life, she mused, are they nice because we compare them to all the ugly, awful things, like threatening winds, crashing stones, and the sun—the sun? And fury, she finished to herself. She spoke aloud, "Is fury such a terrible thing?"

"What, Frances?" Ray answered, sitting, jiggling his sock right-side out.

She leaned at the window. The anger had abated, and Frances looked toward town, past quiet Ann Street with its homes blanched in stillness. Without thinking, she turned to the bed and kissed Ray's cheek, then kissed it again and again, an activity that made so little sense to her that she could not stop, for each kiss was both the beginning of a chance to understand the thing and a way to avoid it.

Ray waited, looking at his shoes. "What will you do

today?" she asked finally.

"Don't know, Frances. Maybe I'll call Kenny. I'll work. I think I'll take a little walk! And I'll make an appointment with Palmer, too—for myself. I think, Frances, that you might do the same."

Frances scowled.

Ray left.

She reached for the telephone, not sure whom to call.

She began dialing her mother's number, and heard a mechanical screeching in the phone, then the sound of folks laughing. Frances sighed and hung up. The phones often malfunctioned in Munson. Lifting, then dropping her arms with sudden fatigue, she recalled, as if from long ago, the deep pleasure of sleep.

As Ray had suggested, Munson was often frustrating. Yet the world beyond it, and beyond Little-Munson, was too complicated to imagine. Considering this idea as a schoolgirl, Frances often had stared at classroom maps.

Her vivacious teacher, Mrs. Cover, had frequently whirled past the students' desks, laughing, hips swinging, dress swishing and suspended from the tension of its crooked seams. Once, reaching out to adjust Frances' undershirt, the teacher chimed gently, "The earth spins round and round, making us nearly sick! The earth knows how to trick us, too, so watch out." Most townsfolk felt similarly, Frances realized, and turned away from the larger goings-on of the world. It—the world—was not for her, nor for anyone in Munson, Frances knew; yet at once, the outer world seemed glamorous and delicious, at least in magazines.

Now Frances sat on a straight chair. In a matter of hours it would be dark, and she expected company for supper. In her cool, half-lit living-room, she waited, ruminating.

When Frances was born, she had had a disorder. Her face had hung strangely, and still did slightly to this day. She had a low eye. Her mouth sagged to one side. The disorder was named after a Belgian doctor, and with it came problems. But fortunately, when Frances was nineteen years old, a young man named Martin French appeared. Martin was a stranger to the town, and so everyone avoided him suspiciously, though he had such a light, smooth air that folks soon forgot themselves and wound up flocking to Martin French after all. As a professional businessman, he inspired respect throughout town, finally; and the newcomer's eyes squinted in such a way when he smiled that he created a sensation—especially with Frances' mother, who told him about electrolysis for the first time in his life.

Martin and Frances met outside the post-office toilet, and there discovered a shy sense of camaraderie. They saw a potential together, and began to keep company. But Frances worried how Martin perceived her. Finally, during a dinner date at the Cove restaurant, she asked, "Martin, what about my face?"

"That's how you are. It doesn't affect me," Martin said, chewing his dinner. Frances smiled to herself, sensing the remark was portentous. Something would come of her friendship with Martin French, she was sure.

When they were married it seemed almost a lark, or, for Frances, a chance to see if everything wouldn't turn out right in life after all. And for a month or two, things were effortless, indeed—just like Martin's smile—requiring so little effort that, in fact, life became featureless to the point that now the period was rather unrememberable. Yet it was not hard to recall the awful thing that happened. In their small apartment at the edge of the beach wall, Frances began to notice that Martin ate large numbers of figs, then later grew gruff and explosive; this became a pattern. And the heart-lifting feeling—the feeling of being saved, which Frances experienced a few months before —disappeared; instead, she sensed a sleek escarpment right next to her. One night, Martin asked her to play a distasteful game, and she refused. On yet another night, he lay pillows on the floor for her to walk upon, as a signal that she should only know softness in life. Frances wondered about the marriage. Sometimes when Martin toweled off near the bathtub, knees bent, arms stretching downward, he seemed feminine, with his diminutive hands and feet. Yet he was unreachably manly as well, protected by the tough barriers of his skin and nose.

Frances had begun to discover the quiet adventure in knowing another human being, and with this came the desire to flee.

Try as she might, she could not know what the marriage meant. She decided to ask her mother about it over a game of cards.

But the mother dragged out the discussion for hours with strange circumlocutions about birds interspersed with sighs of unhappiness: she was not attentive to Frances' concerns. That night, Martin told Frances that he would rather have a heart attack than live with her. She responded, "Could that be because of my face? Or yours?" For it seemed that Martin's face had changed too, and was now beginning to hang lower, like Frances', if only slightly.

"It is not because of anyone's damned face," he yelled.

"I don't know what's happening," she said, and then Martin French tied his robe and left the apartment, never coming back, though at times he called from phone booths.

During this period, Frances sat on the sofa of her old apartment with the westward-facing picture window that took the full brunt of the sun each day and cried to herself. She tried to write down her feelings with a pen, but the pen wobbled too much.

Her mother urged Frances to apply for a job at a small local laboratory to take her mind off the situation. They stood on Frances' porch one night. "Your life is strange," the mother said with distaste, leaning against a beam, cuddling her desiccated fur stole, not minding the heat. "I wonder if you'll always be alone now?"

Frances did not know. In the meantime, keeping busy was a good idea. There were so few jobs in Munson that Frances took the laboratory position, performing the dissection of frozen caterpillars and slicing their tissue with a hand-cranked, circular steel blade.

It was then that her face slowly changed. As she worked long hours in the school lab, the face's sagginess actually began to lift. At moments, she even looked lovely, as an orderly once remarked in the empty cafeteria. At first, the face-shift was imperceptible, though undeniable, and then it became an outstanding fact, though no one mentioned it to Frances once the change was complete.

She considered that the happy, inverted sensation she felt upon first meeting Martin French might merely have been a counterweight to her fear of dying. The ongoing, sickish feelings caused by their onetime alliance compelled her, and she loathed letting this go.

"Why analyze it, Frances?" her sister, Valencia, had said one night, leaning over a steel bowl filled with skinned pears. "Freeze that bastard out of your life, then go down to Ming's for a drink."

Ming was the local tavern proprietor who lived alone at the far edge of Little-Munson, where he tended a family of doves.

"I can't exactly forget Martin. I wonder about him," Frances said.

The sister snorted, then poured a mug of sugar into a mug of water: Valencia liked to experiment with cooking. Valencia was adamant, yet Frances could not be hardhearted. She did not forget Martin French, and sometimes mentioned him—albeit dryly. Her face was now normal, but other things got worse. She lost the ability to sleep well, and took to sitting on the porch at night. Angry skin eruptions began. So did an unpleasant awareness of her womanly side: that she often was making the small, repetitive movements of tidying and storing that were low to the ground, where the edges of things seemed to inveigle her to disappear.

It was as if the disturbance that had caused her face to sag now slid inside her, so that, while her outward appearance improved, another kind of imbalance— a potent one—took its place.

She tried to find a place for herself, and spent a few months associating with a group of young people in town who called themselves "Ears," for they spent their day hours at Ming's tavern, listening to music on a powerful jukebox. Frances pretended to be comfortable with Ears, laughing at their jokes and wearing full, brightly patterned skirts when with them, but deep down, she felt out of sorts. She knew the wild, sessile sensation within her—wind tugging at a rooted tree in her chest—would never go away, and that even as she wished more from life, the wish seemed less negotiable each day.

She asked Palmer, her physician, about these occurrences, and he contextualized the phenomena helpfully by saying, "Frances, sometimes things just happen—and we don't understand why!"

*　　*　　*

Ray and his brother Kenny were due at the house soon, part of the weekly routine for them all. The coffee Frances had made that morning was now a thick slurry of grounds and sugar. From her stool by the stove, she stared down into the pan. How funny it would be if she served this syrupy substance to Ray and his brother! She laughed hard, eyes squeezed shut.

After heating the pot on the tiny, low stove that required her to bend over when cooking, she drank the coffee down. She needed energy. When Ray and Kenny arrived, she would set food out for everyone. Kenny was a fireman.

The telephone rang in long, magnificent peals, and she sprinted to stop the sound, knowing who the caller would be; Frances was unaccustomed to receiving phone calls from anyone besides her mother. "Hello, dear!" She heard a clattering noise behind Mrs. Johnson's voice. Her mother liked to collect wooden oars, and if she bumped into her living-room wall, where the oars hung, they usually fell.

"Mother, I'm busy."

"I wanted to remind you. Please buy a coat, Frances. That wind today was a killer. Winter's coming. I bought a coat for myself today—fireproof!"

"I bought a coat, Mother," she answered. "Leather."

"Oh, for crying out loud! Why did you do that!?" The woman took the news of the coat rather hard. "Of all the coats in the world! But leather! Leather won't protect you from wind or cold! Leather itself is cold. It'll burn, too, and it's not dressy. You've got to think about enhancing your looks—why, at your age, you already have eye-wrinkles. Buy a coat, Frances." The mother hung up.

Frances returned slowly to the kitchen, daydreaming, sitting, recalling the delicious fraud many years ago of feigning illness for a year to avoid school. During that time, she had stayed on her narrow bed for long hours, playing a game of her own invention with cardboard and needles, which had no human opponents and no ending. The plaited silence of the house would thicken; the afternoons were restful and ominous in a way Frances never bothered to ponder.

Once during that year, Frances ran inside the house after watching a low storm move in like a sea. She saw her father sitting at a rough wooden table, eating a freakishly large apple, his head in half-shadow. Then the father stood, winked at her, and went on a trip to a distant city.

When the man returned, his body forming a silhouette in the bright doorway, Frances squinted. He carried a jar filled with green water and small water-creatures from a once-famous lake. Pouring the jar's contents into a tank, the father showed Frances and her siblings the stiff tadpoles, miniature eels, and other tiny fish, explaining that the creatures were known as "foolers," for they were too little to count as real fish at all. The creatures had no organs, and appeared mysteriously in puddles after rain, the father said, simply beginning their existence wherever they saw fit. The fish were eager to live, it seemed.

Frances' mother did not care for the creatures and said so, standing against the hall telephone table. Then Frances and her siblings left the house to sit on the street curb at twilight, waiting, while inside, the mother slowly began to rail against the little fish, building up force, and finally hollering while the father listened, burying her fists in a sofa cushion again and again, repeating that the fish were too wild, too germy, and likely to produce odors. The mother finally put herself to bed while Frances' father dozed in a woolly chair; after supper, Frances woke in her room to see her mother grasping the edge of the doorway with raw, sudsy fingers. "Dammit!" the woman whispered. "I told you I hate those damn fish!"

"Are you afraid?" Frances asked.

"I am not afraid!" the mother shouted, while immediately adding that she feared losing control of herself that night, which she hated, but the fish provoked her as strongly as an allergen, and she could sense them even when she was standing on the roof.

Then Frances watched in her white nightgown as the angrily crying mother rushed across the living-room in bare feet, hoisting the fish tank in her arms, tripping across the rug, and smashing the entire container and its contents down the kitchen sink. Most of the fish slid down the drain, though some struggled in the cut glass mounded in the drain-trap. The mother doused the entire sink area with vinegar and went to bed.

It was not a wholly unique evening for Frances. Yet she wondered what meaning the fish episode had, if any. Hours later, she had not determined one. At sunup she stepped across the kitchen's cold flagstones and scraped her fingertips in the drain, seeking any surviving fish, without success.

Now, Frances shuddered and leaned back on her stool. Stirring the blackish, scalded coffee, she considered her family. Lately, they and other townsfolk had urged her to find a better boyfriend than Ray. "He's not best for you," her mother had advised, while her father stood in the rear hallway of the house, scantly nodding. In a way, Frances thought, it was true. Ray was a bit dull, and he was overfocused on world history. Yet she had no better friend than Ray. Was a better man possible? "Good men—as rare 'round here as pickled hooves!" once joked her aunt, an older woman who had died in bed with her hands in the air.

Many Munson men were bachelors. The same went for Munson women, and the women frequently retired early from work and life altogether. Folks were hesitant about going out; Frances often saw neighbors moving in their homes as shadows behind curtained windows. There were few social events in town: perhaps a wedding every five years, and one annual dance

Frances looked down halfheartedly into a pan of broth.

It was nearly dark. Ray and his brother appeared at the end of Ann Street, walking home, their small, loping steps rhythmic. The screen door slammed.

"Why do you always bring that up?" Kenny, Ray's brother, was saying.

"Because it's damned true," answered Ray. "Why else? You're always coming down with an ailment, be it the sniffles or indigestion." Ray removed his dark, short coat. "Some people are born weak; you were."

"I don't like it when you talk like that!" the fireman cried. "I'm as fit as anyone at the station."

"Nope," Ray replied coolly from a chair.

Kenny took off his shoes and lay back stiffly on the sofa, wiping the thin hair from his forehead. He shut his eyes and inhaled angrily. Then he sat up. "You're in one of those moods, Ray. You think I'm weak? Well, who wanted to drive when we all went to the gorge last year? I did. But no—you insisted on doing all the driving, making Frances and I sit in the back seat like children! I should have forced my point then, but I didn't." He shook his head in great disappointment. "Do you think I like being bossed? Don't you think I want some control over my days and my destiny?"

Ray nearly choked, laughing. "Your destiny! Kenny, you take almost nine years of dawdling and whining before you take the firefighter's test, and you talk about controlling your destiny? God!"

The remark silenced Kenny. Frances sat quietly opposite them with a small green cup in her hand, eyes flickering. She did not care to enter the dispute. Looking through the kitchen doorway and out the back window, she saw small rocks strewn through the grass, and at the rear of the yard, foliage rustled and moved. She sighed.

So many creatures ran there: voles, mice broods, cats as small as the palm of a person's hand. There were litters of other animals, too, running across the yard—and badgers—which were there every night, along with other critters that no one thought of killing, so they ran free in unprecipitated excess and, Frances perceived, a sort of vanity.

She went to the window, straining her eyes to watch the animals surging through the foliage, a river of pelts. She made a face: if she opened the back door, she might detect their odors. Walking to the fireplace, she stooped and wondered aloud, "Is this open?" grabbing the flue handle.

"What did you say, Frances?" Ray asked, leaving the room.

She did not close the flue.

She thought of her own dog, Missie, a terrier, who one night had run from the house and, Frances believed, joined the hordes of animals outside. Missie never had come back. Frances knew Missie was still out there in the wide mantle of bushes that extended from the yard to the alley behind the house, because every so often she would hear Missie's half-bark, or the jingle of the dog's metal collar tag embossed with Frances' name. But for all Frances' whistling and calling, Missie would not come back. There was nothing Frances could do, and though she put a bowl of food in the backyard for the dog every night, which Missie—or something—ate, less and less of the food was consumed as time went on. This indicated to Frances that Missie might be learning to eat a new diet, perhaps one of prey.

"But I miss her so badly!" Frances often told folks when she went shopping in town. And this became a kind of refrain.

Frances looked at Kenny reclined on the sofa, and rubbed her dry hands together.

Kenny said softly, "There's a fellow at the station, Morst—Will Morst. He likes you, Frances."

"Who?" she said numbly.

"Will Morst! You know who I mean. Why don't you come talk to him? We'll have some cookies!"

She looked at Kenny tiredly. "Not another man!" She began to laugh with quiet intensity, bowing over. It was so funny!

"Be quiet, Frances," he said.

"Oh, Kenny." She grew suddenly severe. "I don't like new relationships; they're not my idea of great fun."

"Well, then, what is your idea of great fun?"

She gave him a hard, withering look.

"Frances, just because I try to help you out—! There are men besides my oddball brother, men I'm fond of. You could meet them!"

She stared at him hard. "Kenny, does it ever occur to you that there are ways to mask despair—turn it into vivaciousness and even purpose?"

"Not really. But despair—well, that's—"

"What?" Frances challenged.

"It's a sin!" he posited. Now Kenny seemed rather delighted about something, and sweat shone on his forehead.

"Oh, Kenny, that's old hat." Frances flopped back on the sofa cushion. "I'm not talking about ideas you picked up in the school yard. I'm talking about trying to make it through this life!"

"Make it through life—?" he asked. "What's wrong, Frances? You seem happy enough."

"Happy? Like Curly-Dawn?" she answered in a nasty tone. Curly-Dawn was Kenny's girlfriend.

"What's wrong with Curly?" he said. "She's saving her money. She likes it at the post office." Kenny rose and headed to the kitchen, perhaps seeking a cup of coffee, adding aggressively from there, "At least she's a lady!"

Frances shrugged, coloring, pulling at her skirt.

"She listens to music in her home," he called. "Say, Frances, what kind of show are you running in this kitchen?" He indicated with a finger that the room lacked a kettle, pans, a spice rack, and the like.

She smirked. "Kenny, I need someone to talk to . . . someone very smart!"

"Smarter than me?" Kenny grinned, poking his head back through the doorway.

She sighed. "You're right—I'm not like Curly or the others. I'm different from the girls who walk into town with your fireman friends, all dressed up with sandals. At first it's not noticeable. But the difference is there."

"Yes," Kenny agreed solemnly. "But deep down, you must want to be like them, so as not to be left out. You must want something fresher out of life!"

"Occasionally, I have behaved like the town girls, rushing around downtown, laughing, riding in cars," she mused evenly. "But it never lasts."

He glanced back into the kitchen. "Well, you're young. You'll begin soon. And you don't have to be exactly as those girls are, or wear what they wear, either. Just relax, and the real Frances will shine through!"

She shook with brief, hysterical laughter.

"It's never too late to be a lady," he said, unwrapping a lump of cheese.

Frances thought. Sometimes, coming home from afternoon shopping, she stared at her image in the dark-tinged hallway mirror: the disappointed-looking creature she saw in the skirt and blouse was strange. If she was not a child, then surely she was a type of girl. But she was not a girl, nor was she a married woman, by any means. She had no offspring, and often browsed through boating magazines; with her mouth- and eye-wrinkles she seemed almost an older woman; but she was not. Her belly burned atavistically at times, and she could be aroused upon hearing anyone at all cough or speak her name. What was a girl? Frances never had quite considered herself a full woman; besides, older women were clearly prone to ugliness and illness. She was not that way—not yet. Was she unique?

With a flat expression, she stepped toward Kenny, who held a broken cracker in one hand.

"Kenny, when I was four years old my mother told me, 'You're all alone in the world.' And what do you know: that turned out to be true!"

He stared, then drank down a very small glass of water. "You're a nice girl, Frances. Come meet Will Morst."

A door banged upstairs, and Ray thumped across the upstairs hallway. Another door banged as he headed down the stairs. Frances stared at Kenny dryly. "No," she said with cool, impacted anger.

Kenny gave her a solicitous gaze. "You're not still worried because of your face—from long ago?"

She waved him away. "No, no, it's nothing to do with that. I just don't care to meet Will Morst!"

"How can that be?"

Ray's footstep was in the downstairs back hall.

"Kenny," she said quietly, "I have to talk to you—away from here. Will you meet me later?"

"Oh! Well, sure, if you like—where?"

"Near that barn."

"What barn?

"Out by Rise Road."

"That's not a barn, Frances, it's a legitimate business. It's Hal Arn's motor shop."

"Is that what all those black piles are? Motors?"

" 'Course they're motors. How do you suppose Hal Arn makes his living?"

"All right then—meet me there after you and Ray leave tonight. I want to show you something. If I don't talk to someone soon, I may burst!"

"Gosh. All right, Frances."

She raised her voice. "Can we begin our meal? Please? Ray!" Frances went to a chest of drawers and pulled out a gray tablecloth, shaking it across the table so it billowed, staring at the movement insatiably.

The three drank tea and ate the hard, long, seeded crackers that were so popular in the town. Frances did not much like them, though. Once, she had asked her sister, Valencia, when they were sitting in their mother's kitchen, "Can't we eat something else for a change? I get so tired of these darned things."

"Why can't you be creative? Mash them up with corn and milk, or toast them! You'd be surprised what you can do," Valencia asserted.

Frances had toasted the crackers, but they did not please her. "They're dry," she complained.

Valencia was unconcerned. It was true, she admitted, that a group of men in Munson had once formed a business board, and tried to start some sort of locally based food manufacture. The group met a few times enthusiastically, and even prepared a pamphlet to drum up local interest in the venture. Townsfolk grew excited too, and began to hope for a home industry that, in producing tasty foods, would also promote commerce and draw newcomers to Munson. But then, somehow, folks began to cool on the food manufacture idea, or else forgot about it. Over time, the men stopped going to the meetings, and the business group eventually withered away.

Now Frances glanced at the brothers, who ate their crackers with enjoyment, not noticing her. In the silence she drifted into the kitchen, bringing out further food, and a sauce. If only there were some guarantee, she thought worriedly, that if she left Munson—perhaps Florida altogether—she would not regret it! With rigid fingers she tapped her brow.

Frances left the table to peer quickly inside a book that she kept on the dining table. To its inside cover she had glued a small, inexpensive wristwatch, and this was the only clock in the room. Ray did not care to see clocks in general, since they made him feel rushed, so Frances had pondered until she came up with the idea for the book-clock. It was her own invention, one of which she was quietly proud. Though she had created other domestic inventions, such as a toilet silencer—using rope and soft rags—the book-clock, she felt, was her best.

"Six o'clock," she announced. "You brothers head home! I need time tonight to be alone for mending and what-not." She took a last swallow of tea and scraped her cup along its saucer, eyeing Kenny with a look neither complicitous nor cool.

"God, I understand that!" the fireman cried out, looking at his brother. "So often I need time alone."

Ray bit into a cracker, staring ahead. "Hold it. Let's stay here." He swallowed, then poured more tea. "Did either of you notice the weather late today? Foggy, I thought."

"Ray!" Kenny threw his napkin angrily. "Frances made a request! Didn't you hear?"

"I would like a conversation. Is that a crime?" He raised his eyebrows, so large and glossy, which seemed to live and move separately from him. Ray was in a foul mood, Frances could tell, and during such spells, he was far from accommodating.

They ate some more in silence, and after a time, Ray said, "That fog put me in mind of Austerlitz."

Kenny's face slowly grew pink-red. "You were never at Austerlitz!"

"The fog, along with cannon fire—ha!—sent those autocrats running for their lives," he said. Ray calmly looked at Kenny, who now appeared furious. "Of course I wasn't at Austerlitz. How could I have been? But can't I speculate—for fun? See, Napoleon knew which men to value. He preferred to employ experienced soldiers over the young, inexperienced ones. The failure to do that," Ray said, casting his large eyes, sometimes—now—rather dreamy-looking, to the pinkish living-room wall, "is the absurd flaw of the modern army."

"I think someone better start listening around here," Kenny said vaguely.

"Strong, loyal corpsmen," said Ray, munching, glancing at Kenny as if to provoke fury. "Much better than an overtrained army of youths. The Prussians grew overconfident and idle—we talked about that once, Kenny, remember? The men sat around and overpolished their rifles so much that when they picked them up, the guns exploded in their hands! What is it?" he asked his brother.

Kenny uttered a frustrated, moisture-filled vowel. "Why are you this way? You never listen! You dominate. Can't you see that?"

"Kenny, what's wrong with having a conversation after supper?"

"This isn't a conversation!"

"Oh?"

"If I could get you out of my life—"

"If I could get you out of mine!"

The two stared hard at one another, breathing, their four eyes gleaming brown. "But we have to be together," Ray said then, slowly, evenly, sitting back, "because we're brothers."

"Hurry up and eat, dammit," Frances broke in. She was anxious for them to leave so she and Kenny might meet later. Ray finished his meal, lifting his eyebrows toward her.

*　*　*

Frances rode the bicycle with difficulty, maneuvering on the path in a wobbly fashion, her face squeezed hard, as though with unrockable thoughts and convictions. Since she had not slept well the past several nights, her bike-riding was sloppy, and she fell; as a consequence, her hand was bloodied by the time she leaned the bicycle against the side of Hal Arn's motor shop. The night air was dazzlingly cold, and slick, muddy leaves stuck to her hard shoes. A voice remembered from long ago rose in her mind:

"I wouldn't go into the forest at night, not if I were you. I'd keep well to the path and beware the cunning of the trees. I wouldn't trust the path, not for a moment, if I were you. Pay heed to this! I once knew a girl who . . ."

It was the voice of the older aunt, who had often frightened Frances with talk of peril.

She heard a step. "Oh, Frances!" Kenny exclaimed, rushing to her with an outstretched handkerchief, seeing the gashed hand. Ineffectually, he daubed at the wound; when the handkerchief grew stained, he twisted it upon itself, then poked it nervously up his sleeve.

"Does that hurt?"

" 'Course it hurts," she snapped. "But the pain's not going to stop just because I want it to, is it? Kenny, I have to talk to you."

He bit his lip. "Is it because you want to leave Ray, Frances?"

"Good night! That's not it. —Kenny, do you remember when we all went on a hayride?"

"You mean last fall? Seth Meagre went crazy that night. They took him to Health Hall for an evaluation and he never—"

"What else happened that night, Kenny?" Frances interrupted.

"I don't know . . . that meeting to shut down the beaches and roads?"

"No, that was another time."

"I don't remember. Oh, what's the matter, Frances?" He fumbled in his pocket, pulling out another handkerchief already covered with a heavy stain, perhaps ink, and, after holding this cloth near Frances' face for a moment, perhaps offering, he stuffed it into his sleeve behind the first handkerchief, creating a crinkled knot.

"Something must've happened that night," she said.

"Why, for heaven's sake?"

"Because ever since then, Kenny, I've had a scar."

His eyes widened.

"Tell me what you think." She raised her woolen skirt to reveal a clumpy mass of tissue on her thigh. The scar actually seemed to be formed of clusters of smaller scars bearing a resemblance to boils, and dried, black blood lined its crevices. The scar appeared to spread out uncontrollably from a center point, as if it were not a scar, but a disease. It was unpleasant to look at.

"Jesus, Frances!" Kenny exclaimed angrily, as if the disfigurement were her fault. He stepped back. "Have you washed that?"

"I have."

"What the hell is it?"

"I don't know! Kenny," she went on shakily, "that night I wanted to feel something I'd never felt. Oh, I wished for it like mad!"

"Wished for what?"

"Well . . . for something new. A new sensation, or a whole new life, maybe. I wished for something to overpower me!"

"Why, Frances. How strange!"

Her voice became quieter, more frantic. "But Kenny!

Doesn't everyone like to be overpowered now and again?"

He glanced away.

"I couldn't sleep for thinking about it. Do you think this mark came up on my leg that night for no reason except that I wished for those things?"

"Gee, you wouldn't think so." Kenny examined the wound. "But you never know. You said it happened the night of the hayride. How do you know that?"

"That's when I first saw it. Kenny, I wished for something else that night."

"What?"

"To leave Munson."

"Leave? Why?" Kenny was incredulous.

"Why do you think?"

"To find something awfully new and different?" he guessed.

"Dammit! To leave Munson and all its maladies— mine—behind!" She balled her fists, then released them. "But what happened, Kenny? I got a brand-new malady! My life has been difficult, you know; this town doesn't help."

Kenny squeezed his pale fingers, one after the next. "Aren't all lives difficult, Frances?"

She tore on. "Kenny, don't you see? It's Munson! There is something in the air here, a kind of pressure. Don't you feel it? The way folks look at you, judging, when you walk by. The way they stare, then criticize! You know how no one wants to be the first one to go outside in the morning? And why do they say 'Choose well,' instead of a simple 'Goodbye'?"

"Oh," Kenny waved her off. "That's just a few older

folks. Timeworn customs aren't bad, Frances. They help teach us things that are true."

Frances was familiar with this remark, having heard it in her childhood many times. "But Kenny, what can we learn that's so true? In other towns, things are different."

"I doubt it. Listen, we are just a small, harmless village where folks work hard. Watch what you say, Frances! Munson is your home."

"Kenny," she clipped his shoulder angrily. "People are frightened here! But of what?"

He thought, shaking his head.

"The way they peek out their windows in their pajamas! On the street, folks whisper negative sorts of judgments about me and my life, I know it! Oh, something's going to burst in me! I can't sleep. Something's got to change."

Exhaustion unwound inside her, and she looked to the ground, with its profusion of mudworms. "Kenny, d'you think a town can slowly smash a girl by dismantling her personality in dozens of small ways?"

The sound of her voice strained into the dank air, seeming to become part of the massive precipice of night. Frances waited, looking around, wondering momentarily how any two entities, such as molecules or atoms, could endure the experience of fusion without shock.

"Well, I never thought about that," Kenny answered at last. "Frances, I'm sorry about your scar."

She pressed her gaze into him, now holding his arm in its blue sweater, an act that gave her sparse comfort, and Frances was unable to stop the impulse to look at Kenny pleadingly. Far off, she heard a mild crunching or squeaking, the sound of insects or bees closing in—it was certainly possible, she imagined—on something of great value.

"At the station, you know, Frances, we have our Captain, Tod Maria," he said. "Tod's not a bad sort. He's cheerful."

Frances smirked.

"Once, though," Kenny went on, "during evening circle, Maria sounded the way you sound tonight. A little worried, you might say. A little wild in the mind. That night, he told me he was afraid he would split in two!"

"Split in two?" She breathed in wonder. "But why?"

"Because of problems," Kenny replied promptly.

"Oh, dammit!" she turned and spat. "Don't you see? This town makes a mess of people! Why don't folks understand? They get so mixed-up here. Kenny, why shouldn't I leave?"

"It wouldn't be worth it," Kenny pointed out. "Munson's part of you. And it's not so different from the rest of the world as you'd like to believe."

"If it's not so different, then leaving will be all the easier!"

"Frances," he chastised. "Think of Josh White. Think of Selma Mather."

Selma Mather had been a classmate of Frances' with a lazy eye who, even as a little girl, always had pined for men in general, and especially for men from larger, more sophisticated locales. Selma was afraid her wish would never become real. One afternoon, though, when in her young twenties, Selma ran through Munson's streets with high spirits and mud on her legs, because behind her she pulled a fun-loving soldier who had been passing through town on a truck. The town was concerned, but soon grew accustomed to the sight of Selma Mather parading the soldier through the streets; besides, it was understood that once Selma relaxed, the couple could marry. A wedding was arranged, including preparations for a lawn-sized cake.

But peculiarly, Selma could not calm down. She continued to careen along Munson's streets, much too giddy, laughing too hard, both with the soldier and without him, chatting feverishly and far into the night about her future and the marriage until some folks began to talk as if Selma Mather were growing ill. She had acquired an imbalance, some said. The young woman did not look right, either, having acquired a gaunt look and a grayish stain at the side of her neck. Seven days after finding the man, Selma Mather was killed by a tree falling on her head and spine, and though folks whispered that the soldier had not really been a soldier, but in fact a robber, it was clear that he had not killed Selma Mather. The man departed town as easily as he had entered, bouncing his rucksack, not caring to stay.

In a gesture unfamiliar to Frances, Kenny preened his hair with a finger. "You have to think about your future, you know."

"What the hell does that mean?"

"You have responsibilities—both to townsfolk here, and yourself. Most girls your age wouldn't mystify everyone, or let the town down by leaving. And it would be hard to go away, Frances. Do you really want to wake up in an unfamiliar room and feel nauseated besides? New places affect the digestion, you know."

"True," she admitted uneasily.

"And that scar of yours!" he pointed. "I'd worry about

traveling with that. Frances, would you like to come meet Tod Maria?" he added softly. "You'd like him, I think. Naturally, he's very protective of the ladies he cares for."

"Oh, Kenny!" she cried sourly. "Tod is so large! Why do you always try and bring me to men?"

"I don't know . . . I just can't seem to settle with the way you are. Besides, why should my brother be allowed to have you?"

Kenny waited. He looked down at her with a strong expression, drawing close. "Frances . . . you ask me to come way out here at night to show me a scar on your leg, and you tell me that you're looking for a new sensation in life. What am I supposed to think?"

Frances raised a grin; the grin trembled. A knot of tension lifted in her chest, and she fell to Kenny because it seemed she must, kissing him in great, long, inhalatory movements, as if these breaths could pull her through the episode more quickly. Kenny's arms dropped, then wandered behind him awkwardly for a moment, reaching as if for a ballast.

The kiss felt strange, membranous to Frances, and as he reached for her, she stepped away, saying, "Kenny, don't touch my hair or arms."

"Why not?"

"I don't care for it, that's why not." She stared to the barn area and its syrupy surrounding darkness.

"Things in this town simply happen, arising out of nowhere," she said.

He looked up at the sky's star-specks. "I suppose."

"In that same manner, I will leave Munson," she stated airily. "Out of the blue, I'll leave. I'm on edge here, Kenny. Besides, I've never liked . . . well, my you-know."

Kenny nodded.

Frances was referring to the fact that, every month or so, she kept appointments with her physician to address an old medical ailment that was both awkward and embarrassing.

The first treatment had occurred during Frances' early teenage years. At that time, her mother and older sister also received the treatment from the doctor, and they encouraged Frances to do the same. However, the sister grew abruptly angry about something Frances did not understand and abandoned the treatment, going to settle at the farthest possible edge of Munson—beside an old mud lake—with a man, a barrel-maker who disliked cities and towns, and to this day, Valencia led quite a separate life. Meanwhile, Frances' mother became cooler toward the doctor, saying her heart was in poor shape, and she stopped the treatments as well. Only Frances continued to see the old physician regularly through the years, and when he died, she continued the treatments with Palmer, in part because she felt the treatments were an obligation she must keep.

"You oughtn't leave Munson suddenly, Frances," Kenny insisted. "You'd better not! It's plain crazy."

"Go away now, Kenny. It's time for me to think."

His voice was serious. "When someone leaves a town, it's terrible. The people left behind can't get back on their feet."

Frances said nothing.

He lingered, then drifted off, voice stabbing into the sky's cold margin beyond the barn. "All right, then, if you think you're so free and wonderful, go ahead and leave! You'll see where it gets you!" Kenny drew an angry breath, then raced away, his thin figure blurred blue.

* * *

Frances pushed her bicycle home. The air was no longer cold, nor did it seem warm, but instead neutral, without temperature. Frances was regretful. For the second time in a day, she had failed to understand a kiss. "I lack a certain resolve," she stated aloud.

What would happen if she left Munson? Frances was unable to imagine this scenario, or life in another town. Kenny was probably right, though: it would be unpleasant. Ray wouldn't want her to leave Munson either, she knew.

What did Frances Johnson want?

Tiny, seedlike insects moved upon the ground below her, endlessly methodical, affording her a sensation of comfort, for she felt an affinity with things that crawled or hid. Lice were not destructive and had the power to mimic other phenomena, for example, teardrops on a kitten's face; and insects had a kind of unchallenged power, for example, to step freely into any person's home unpunished, since they did not understand the boundaries of human property. Yet to Frances, such creatures were not purely innocent either, and this thought caused her heart to drum with hope.

When Frances was an older teen, she met someone, a woman, with whom she began to have discussions. The discussions became frequent, and over time, almost fulfilling, because the woman listened so well, her brown eyes absorbing all: it made Frances feel as giddy as if she were swimming in a pool, uncertain if the water's surface was above or below her head. The woman's name was Nancy, and with her, Frances would often laugh for almost no reason, and loudly. Nancy sported sure talents, along with the thickest glasses Frances had ever seen. Her house was surrounded by a dwarf ivy composed of hundreds of thousands of minuscule leaves, and over the years, as Frances continued talking with Nancy, it became clear that the two had grown fond of each other, and then Nancy retired.

Nancy was a mother, but Frances did not know to whom. Even so, Nancy had been close at hand when Frances had had her first period, long ago. Frances hadn't wanted to tell Nancy, but she did, because she needed a pad, so she biked the miles to Nancy's place, asking for one.

"Why do you want a pad, dear?" Nancy had asked. Perhaps Nancy thought she was playing a game.

Frances didn't answer, but just shook her head and looked to the floor, so then Nancy knew. She got up from her chair, hugged Frances, and yelled, "You're a lady!"

"Why be so darned cheerful about it?" Frances huffed. "I don't want to change or become someone new. I'm fine the way I am."

Nancy joked, "Do you imagine that girls turn into monsters at the onset of womanhood?" and then the two fell silent.

Frances cried, finally, for the thought of being womanly was awful, perhaps a route to becoming uncontrolled and making large, sloppy, splaying motions of the arms and legs, or the beginning of a lifetime of dull, colorless skin and throaty laughter; certainly it was the beginning of the path to death. And standing there in her flattering suit and pumps, Nancy cried too, for, she admitted, being a woman was an experience rife with tension, aggravation, and shame that continued unabated. They cried together, even while Nancy whispered that they had become overly nostalgic over a lie, that of the purity of girlhood.

"But it's not a lie," Frances insisted. "Don't most little girls simply live happy, contented lives?"

"Hell, no!" Nancy clamored, startling Frances. The woman told her that little girls—even those who played not with dolls, but with hard plastic soldiers and games of war and insurrection—generally lived secretly, separately from the world, moving as if upon a river of glass, unseen.

Nancy's quiet living-room, with its shoeboxes, dust, and crumb-littered rug, seemed a haven: Frances wanted never to leave.

Once, Frances got angry with Nancy. They argued. Frances stood up dramatically, as if to rush from the room. Indeed, Nancy cried out, "Wait!" and stood, unsteady on her high shoes, one hand outstretched, straightening her flowered skirt with the other. She threw Frances a complicated gaze. "You would like very much for me to chase you right now, wouldn't you?" she asked, and Frances stared dumbly. Nancy gave forth a gentle, equine laugh. "Little children like to make their parents chase them," she noted, "in play, because chasing is a form of assurance and love. Is that what you would like?" Frances nodded at last, hotly ashamed.

Since that day, Frances had behaved rather sheepishly around Nancy; in any case, she had never been the type to snake her arms around anyone's torso at all, even Ray's, in a warm embrace. She never wished to hug Nancy, except for one night, when she did.

Ray did not seem to notice or mind Frances' nondemonstrativeness, since he was often busy with projects. And at night, the prospect of a love-experience made Ray's eyes turn to flat, wooden discs as he moved away. Frances admitted to herself that she was much the same. In any case, Ray had never seemed overly infatuated with Frances; instead, he focused his admiration on other people, for example, Napoleon and various generals.

Walking along the dust-heaped, barely distinguishable road, neither moon nor clouds above, Frances squeezed the bicycle's handlebars, giggling, recalling a joke Nancy had once made about garden peas. She was sure her parents would like Nancy and admire her tasteful skirts. Had she and Nancy grown apart? Frances could not remember the last time she had talked to the woman. "Lately, I think of her often. I must see her again!" she vowed, the words flying from her evaporatively; and she suddenly recalled the pebbled, feather-piled road to Nancy's isolated house, which was also dense with a certain breed of snail. The house itself was a wide structure that looked, at least from the outside, luxurious, though it had no gutters.

But first, Frances had to find Palmer.

*　　*　　*

"I haven't the faintest idea what it is."

Frances lay back on the exam table in Palmer's office, looking to the ceiling, considering what the doctor said as he cheerfully tapped her scar's outer penumbra with a paper clip, then went to wash his hands.

"Well,"—Palmer　let　a　little　giggle　escape　his

throat—"that's not entirely true. I have a notion about it. We can talk, if you like, in a few minutes." He wrinkled his long nose and his pale, oblong face seemed to shine. "What about the other?" He was referring to the condition that amounted to little more than extremely frequent, burning urination.

Lying on the table, Frances turned her head away. She had not come to Palmer's office today because of that condition, and did not want to discuss it.

When Frances first met Palmer a year or so before, he wore little wire glasses and, beneath his lab coat, tight, pinkish pants that may have been fashionable either somewhere outside of Munson, or during another era. Munson's town council had struggled to find a new physician for the region, because old Doctor Frann, the silent, hoary physician of the mustard-colored skin whom Frances had known all her life, had died while napping in the woods.

Palmer arrived to town good-naturedly, though folks did not care for the stranger's manner or clothing. But Palmer carried at all times a letter written to him in his childhood by a distant relative who, decades before, had lived and died in Munson. Over time, skittish townsfolk—Frances, her mother, and sister included—began to accept the doctor.

Now, Palmer's clothing fitted more loosely, and his glasses were box-shaped. Continuing the tradition with the old doctor, Frances saw Palmer regularly for the procedure her mother had advocated years before. Sharply painful, but over so fast that the pain amounted to something ineffable, the treatment seemed to help slightly. When Frances had endured the procedure's discomfort last month, wincing, Palmer shook his head slowly, exhaling, but she did not understand why.

Now Palmer stood before her, smiling, arms dangling; a quality of suspension befell the room. In a moment, he was gone. Frances rested tiredly on the exam table, drawing in air, hearing him enter another exam room down the hall, saying reproachingly, "Now, Mrs. Best . . ." Slowly, Frances rose from the table, recalling a solid sack of sugar that leaned against her damp basement wall at home. She dressed carefully, and after some minutes tiptoed from the exam room through the hallway, passing Palmer's small office crowded with stacks of paper, books, and slithery magazines. The doctor was sitting at his desk. As she passed, to Frances' surprise, he raced to the doorway, hand extended, calling. "Frances, Frances—come have a seat! Come in!" His glasses were askew, and the hand held a buttered cracker, gesturing for her to sit down.

He sat, tugging at the hem of the short lab coat that scantly covered his hips, smiling boyishly, chewing, shrugging. "How goes life?" he asked.

Frances faced the doctor with discomfort, imagining that he perceived everything: her worries, her attempts to hide these, and the vulnerable surface of her mind that rippled with sensations of flight.

She was lost.

"How's your fellow—Ray—isn't that his name?"

"Fine." The office, with its insulation of books and paper, compacted the sound of her voice.

The doctor laughed softly, as if automatically. "Life is full of drama!" he offered, setting the cracker on a plate. "Actually, I prefer comedy to drama; drama bothers me," he rattled on. "Yet we can't avoid it, even in Munson."

He leaned forward. "Not that it's any of my business, Frances. But . . . ! I've been wondering. In my year here, I've never seen people chat together in my waiting-room. For that matter, I've never seen neighbors host a little get-together in someone's backyard! Why is that?"

Palmer's question put Frances in the position of defending the town, which she did not like. "We have parties, all right. I suppose you just don't know about them."

"Oh? I don't quite believe that!" The doctor faced her, chin sunk into his folded hands, a merry challenge in his eyes. "I think I would have heard about a little party here and there."

"Well . . . we have a dance once a year, anyway. Do other towns host such frequent, wonderful parties, by comparison?"

"Sure they do."

"Well, how darned marvelous can a party be, Palmer? It's just a matter of a few hours, then everyone goes home."

He wiped his hands of crumbs. "Yes, in a way, you are right. I recall parties from California that were dull, and some that were disastrous! Those were strange days for me, Frances, with a strange odor to them."

Palmer's small desk and its dented green metal depressed Frances, making her recall dour rain.

"We're quiet here in Munson, and we work hard," she said at last, guardedly, "because we have potent responsibilities." Then she realized with withering despair that these were the exact words of Enoch Ruth, the town's council leader, who, during her childhood years and beyond, made frequent speeches and warnings to the town.

"What responsibilities are those?" Palmer asked, but Frances could not seem to answer.

"I have duties too, and every evening I work at home, trying to invent a new compound that the world has never seen before, but Frances, I still find time to relax!"

She frowned. "Are you saying that the people of Munson have a chip on their shoulder?"

"I'm saying it a little."

She answered coolly, eyes flat. "We keep to ourselves, that's all. We work hard."

"Hmm," Palmer breathed critically.

Frances suppressed a sob, then released it. She was, she realized, merely thinking of her dog.

"Ah. At times, I feel regret too, Frances," the doctor offered.

She sniffed. "Has your regret to do with a woman, Palmer?"

"Ha-ha!" The man smiled, not answering further, his glasses crooked on his nose so comically that Frances gave forth a sharp, sudden laugh. It came to her for the first time since Palmer arrived to town that he might not be a bad sort, and something in her mind leapt toward his water-green eyes. With their measure of humor, alongside his rough, flaking face-skin, he looked, Frances thought, like an earnest teacher, or the type of dreamer who owns an ice-cream shop.

As the afternoon passed, Frances examined the papers, torn ledgers, and disease journals piled in the close office, and the sun shifted such that a weak angle of light passed through the tiny, high window, gently warming her face, imparting a panoply of sensations from vigor to distress.

Looking at the doctor again, she recalled the

threatening, windy sky earlier that morning and the wide, straw-strewn fields beside his office. It would be night soon. Frances was weary. Gauzily, she imagined an ideal future in which she would not be tired, but instead surrender at all times to a magical, devouring sleep that would subsume her life's days entirely.

Would Frances Johnson find a way?

Her sleeplessness weighed on her mind, possibly as a topic to discuss with Palmer, yet there were so many things to discuss. On any given day in Munson following the volcano's rumblings, townsfolk seemed to grow energetic and enthusiastic—perhaps too enthusiastic—about life: Frances did, too. Did Palmer know? On those days, she, like other folks, would throw open her bedroom window wide to breathe more daytime air, or chatter with the town's phone operators. She would make careful, excited, detailed plans for home inventions, reading, sewing, and for the boldest project of all—packing and leaving Munson for good. But soon enough, as with other folks too, her energy would falter, and none of the plans would begin, let alone come to fruition.

Palmer was reading from a paperback book on his desk, scratching his ears one at a time.

She blurted, "Palmer, I've got to leave Munson."

He leaned onto his elbows. "Gee! You'd be one of the few. Locals leave Munson just about as frequently as they have parties, eh?"

"Are you saying it would be wrong to go?" She looked at the open door, sensing that someone might be near, listening.

He waved her off. "Of course not! Frances, if you desire this, why, it might be a wise and healthful choice."

Feeling a glow in her throat, she exhaled a warm, glad breath, and smoothed her hair toward the man flirtatiously. "Oh, that's a nice thing to say, Palmer . . . but . . . d'you suppose I can make a journey with this scar on my leg?"

"I don't see why not. You see, the phenomenon is not unfamiliar to me."

"You recognize the scar?"

He frowned. "I've seen it before. They called it, simply, 'cauliflower' at the seaside medical college where I trained. Where there's one case, there's many." He turned to the high window. "My, wouldn't it be nice to sit up there in one of those fruit trees?"

"Palmer! You mean others in town have the same scar as I?"

"Sure, maybe." The man raised his eyebrows. "Probably lots of cases in Little-Munson, too."

"But—can it be passed?" She felt frantic.

"Oh, Frances. Yes, some bacteria can leap from one person to another—you know that—remember how this fact was conveyed so beautifully in the old horror movie *Friendless*? However, in this case—" Palmer removed his glasses.

Frances was on her feet. "Palmer! Did I catch this scar from someone? From—Ray, do you mean to say? Not really!?"

"Oh, be quiet," he muttered, grasping a pencil in awkward fingers, unwilling to offer reassurance. Frances waited, anxiously glancing up to the window, the smallness of which now seemed absurd.

"I wonder if the earth was ever truly harmonious?" the man inquired of himself.

"The scar is so ugly. What could it mean?"

A heap of slick magazines suddenly poured from his desk and onto the floor. "Must it mean something? Why does a wart appear, Frances? Why did the dinosaurs, so long ago? And why did the dinosaurs die, anyway? Where did the earth and its moon begin?" A small thrill of peril passed through Frances, for the chaos of it.

"Illnesses and other phenomena arrive without explanation, like miracles," the man huffed, his longish face growing longer, "or anti-miracles. And of course, there was the day that each of us arrived, too."

She was quiet.

"And to know the meaning of it? The meaning is a waste of time," he said.

"If people," she remarked slowly, calmer now, thinking, "get mysterious illnesses . . . well, maybe entire towns can acquire illnesses, too!"

He smiled slowly, revealing rows of teeth which, she noticed for the first time, were disturbingly small. "Oh, Frances, you are a delight. Yes, indeed, an entire town may be ill, in its way. I do agree!"

Doctor and patient now looked at one another with bright interest.

"Palmer," she began. "About the treatments I received from old Doctor Frann . . . the ones I still get from you. For example, last month . . ."

"Yes?" He swiveled around in the chair.

"Well, I don't like them!" she said, surprising herself. "They hurt, and they're embarrassing too. Can't we stop?"

The man giggled. "Well, certainly! That procedure is outdated and useless, anyway. Why did you want it in the first place?" He switched on a small transistor radio.

She was dumbfounded. "But, Palmer . . . why did you agree to perform the procedure, if it's useless?"

The doctor gazed downward with a troubled expression, as if lost.

"Have you changed recently, Frances?" he asked at last, in a faint voice.

Frances knew she had. It was many years ago when she first attended the old physician's office, holding her mother's hand, packed with a burning, nervous worry she worked hard to ignore. Afterward, at home, she had gone into her parents' cellar, lay on a cement pallet, and stared through the numerous holes of a pegboard, willing an unnamed injury, a rawness inside her, to fly through the peg-holes and away from the earth.

With a timid smile, Palmer spoke again. "I wouldn't worry about this scar business, Frances. I don't think the condition will worsen. Don't show your scar to the townspeople, though: that's my advice. It may make them uneasy. Besides, what are you going to do? Walk downtown and shout, 'Hey, does anybody have a big scar?' Oh, me." He laughed, slapping the desk edge, wiping tears. Shuttering his eyes then, he rocked with feeling to the thin, tuneless radio music, wiping his hair.

Frances stood.

"Avoid heavy foods—these may cause corns," the doctor said in summation. "Drink water, but never the poison that is orange juice. Use fatted soap," he added, fingering a magazine, glancing at it.

As Frances left the office, she looked back at Palmer, who picked up a pale glass marble from his desk, examining it carefully, as if for wens.

*   *   *

Atop her bicycle, Frances passed near the border of Little-Munson, gazing at the open wiring of its buildings and car parts strewn across a lot. A smart collection of hoses lay in an adjacent lot. Little-Munson, so tiny, so dependent on Munson for its goods, sheriffs, and other essentials, sported only one unnamed main street, with a few other dusty streets intersecting it. At night, a cloudy orange glow from lights above an abandoned gasworks made the town look fiercer, larger than it was. A low, long building like a bunker ran the length of the main street, extending into the sand dunes beyond Little-Munson's limits, where yellow hills amounted to little more than a smallish desert that was nonetheless damp during many months of the year. Frances thought she heard a yelp from within the bunkerlike building: she knew that folks lived inside.

As a tradition, most Munson folks had no interest in Little-Munson residents, and few in Little-Munson had the desire to seek out their Munson neighbors, either. It was as if each town preferred to deny that the other existed. But once, Ray had had a friend, Happy Jaine, who occasionally worked in front of Munson's only bakery, and oddly, he had hailed from Little-Munson. The bakery itself was well-known throughout Munson, yet, in a way, it was never enjoyed wholeheartedly, for while its main office was located in Munson, its ovens were situated in a building that actually sat upon the Munson/Little-Munson boundary. Happy in particular did not like this, because he always wanted to forget Little-Munson.

In those days, Happy lived full-time in Munson and

swept bread crumbs, seeds, and other debris from the bakery's pavement; he was an elfin, social, tidy man with knoblike knees and a full grin above his broom. Once, in her first year with Ray, Frances had been feeling outgoing, and as she had passed Happy near the bakery, she clipped him on the shoulder rather hard, then smiled such that Happy Jaine immediately led her behind the bakery's oven-building, over a guardrail, and into a meadow crowded with torn bags and a colony of rabbits. Frances was wary of Happy, who remained silent; she stepped carefully, for she was accustomed to rabbits, though she did not care for their long minutes of stillness or brindled bodies.

She looked up to Happy, wishing to like him, knowing the man was firm in his opinions and could be very stern. Happy chewed a root, staring at her. Frances fidgeted, then finally burst into a terribly nervous smile with an accompanying honk of laughter, for she had begun to imagine—and nearly believe—that after this meeting with Happy, her life would change without her consent, and that it would, from this moment on, revolve solely around Happy Jaine and his life and concerns. Helplessly, she saw her future busy and full of motion, beginning and ending always with Happy, the ups and downs of his job, his preferences, and his tough, wiry beard.

The man prodded a dozing rabbit with the toe of his shoe, then spoke, coincidentally, about the very thing Frances was pondering: the future.

"Years from now, the world will improve from the state it is in today," he explained, "but not before a disaster happens. Times are getting so tough that in a few years, people will be forced to give up their fancy home heating and mouthwash, and they won't have anyone to cry to. See, the people of today are lazy, Frances, because they're soft and lost their backbone. They'd rather have a lot of comfort and pampering than getting prepared for the worst, like me. Someday they'll see I was right. Florida's lazy habits will disappear."

She did not follow his train of thought. "Do you like comfort, Happy?" she asked, and the man narrowed his eyes at her, smiling, as if to chastise.

To break the long silence and eye contact, Frances spoke again. "Have you ever been outside the state, Happy?"

He chewed the root more actively. "You play your cards right, Frances. That's your ticket to a better life in this world. I'm always careful to play my cards right."

"You are?"

"It's fifteen years since I left Little-Munson by my wits alone, and I wouldn't go back there for money."

"But you are in Little-Munson now, Happy; we're both here, more or less, because the bakery's oven-room is partly there, and partly—"

"You idiot! That's not what I mean!" Happy thundered. But the man's fury soon changed, and he looked down at Frances, ready for a full kiss. She looked up at him with shining eyes, as she knew she should, sensing with disappointment for Happy that she was not really the girl she should be for him, though he did not know it.

Who could Frances Johnson be?

Smiling to him, trying hard, Frances existed partially. Her hands and mouth working as if to rudder herself, she kissed Happy, catching a scent of some sweet-sour esculence in the air around them, which she judged to be a flavor perhaps in the recesses of Happy's body itself. The kiss slid around her face like a wet rubber ring, and Happy said again, though in a softer tone, "Play your cards right, Frances," as the kiss incited in her a steamy, unpleasant sensation. To answer Happy's remark, she could think of nothing more than to smile and instigate another long, crawling kiss; and after some time she was able to convince the man that she must go home to her mother, who would be waiting by the telephone.

Now, Frances wondered rotely if Happy Jaine had managed to avoid returning to Little-Munson before he died, even though it had been his home. As she steered the bicycle toward the yellow sand-hills, past Little-Munson's broken warehouse and still-functioning waterworks, she tasted the salty-dust air, hearing behind her another yelp inside the long bunkerlike building, then the same voice resonating with laughter.

Local wisdom said folks in Little-Munson were divided about things and agitated by nature, while those in Munson were clear-sighted and straightforward. Yet some people—Nancy among them—said the reverse was actually true. Little-Munson once had had a robust police force, but at some point it had fallen apart; now any policing was done by Munson's sheriffs. This intrusion caused tension in Little-Munson, though it could be argued that the town scarcely existed anymore. Were the people there truly unlucky? A few years ago, she learned that Happy's had been a quick, unusual death from a combination of snake-bite and falling off a rock ledge, and this had not much surprised Frances.

She pedaled the bike onto an ocean road blocked at its far outlet by a wooden barrier that Munson had erected many years before. The local volcano was dangerous, signs on the barrier informed, and went on to say that Munson's town council had reason to believe the sea-water touching the volcano's base was dangerous, too. Though the beach barriers were in place, Munson folks needed no reminding; they stayed away. Over the years, the wooden barricade had fallen into disrepair, chewed by destructive insects or torn apart by teens.

Frances' bicycle tires pressured the fine sand, and it sprayed upward, stinging her eyes. As she reached the beach barrier, she stopped the bike, sighing, tired. A movement in the bare brush caught her attention, and she looked up to see a fuzzy, mild-faced critter at some distance, which was actually a type of bear. The animal pushed out of the bushes and loped along the road, its heavy forearms swaying rather comically. Frances felt timid. She caught the critter's watery, dark gaze for a moment, then sped off, retracing her route, impatient to reach Nancy. She headed for a certain path that dipped back briefly toward Little-Munson while also offering a series of sliverlike trails that led some distance away, skirting both towns, fading to nothing. The path also merged with a larger, more legitimate road altogether, and finding that route at last, she pedaled off.

It might be too dark now to visit Nancy, Frances realized with disappointment. Daytime would be best for that. At a bend in the road, through foliage overgrown with sodden tree-fluff, she turned off and crested a hill, pushing the bike tiredly until, in the distance, she saw a familiar cafe. The air hinted at rain. Frances saw a lone taxi buzzing toward Munson so quickly that the driver appeared faceless, his thin sleeve rippling in the wind.

Now hungry, Frances trudged up the gravel driveway to Mal's Pico Diner and parked her bicycle. A girl in a mint-green dress rushed to serve a plate of crackers and butter as Frances sat, then the girl moved silently behind the counter, pulling a box of frozen food from a hamper and throwing its contents into a metal well for frying.

"It will be ready in a moment," the girl said, and while the food boiled, the girl began to cry. She disappeared into the kitchen, came back, and standing again beside the fryer, cried rather softly into the crook of her arm. Frances felt vaguely at fault and wished for the girl to go home to bed, though she blurted out, "Drink a glass of water!" which sent the girl into a wrenching storm of fur-ther tears before she fled to the kitchen through a swing-ing door. Some minutes later, the cook, a man in a dirty smock, emerged. He shook the food from its basket onto a plate, which he set before Frances.

"That waitress—" Frances began.

"She's jes' that way," said the cook, and returned to the kitchen.

Staring at the yellowish food, then at the cafe around her, Frances struggled inside herself. The place was too empty. No longer hungry, she raised herself from the booth and straightened her skirt, lonely, wiping her nose, and she pushed through the same door as had the girl and the cook.

The kitchen's long, warped, diagonal cutting board extended far to the rear of the building alongside a table that also seemed indefinitely long. A light-bulb hung overhead. The cook stood behind the stove, squinting; he wore a blank name-tag on his smock. Behind him a smallish teen boy with light hair sat on a milk crate, eating slowly and absorbedly from a bowl of mush.

"Hello!" Frances cried loudly.

The cook looked at her, smoking.

"I went to see Palmer today," she told him conversationally.

The old cook leaned on the cutting board, looking through the pass-through and into the cafe. "Th' doctor?"

"That's right."

The cook waited, eyes moving, seeming to recall something.

"He said I've got a scar."

"Th' doctor did."

"Yes, and he said other people in town certainly may have them, too!"

"Got a scar, eh?"

"That's right."

"Got a big scar on the belly, don' ya?"

"Oh, no, nothing like that—it's on my leg," she replied.

"I'll tell you," the cook said, squinting, grabbing up a metal spatula from the stove, tapping it on the grill, "that's no scar, Missy. That's a tumor."

The room seemed to spin for Frances, and she placed her hand on the cool refrigerator door. "How do you know that? Did you hear something in town?"

"Mebbe I did, mebbe I didn't." The cook paused, leaning on a stove. "Doesn't hurt, does it?"

"No."

"And it came up real silent-like, right?'

"I don't know. I just noticed it one day!"

"Tha's right. You listen t' me. Paul Buster out at

the water tower had one of them tumors. He cut it off hisself, with his car key. Go out an' see him. He'll tell you. Yeah, lotta people get them tumors, all the ladies, most 'specially."

"What ladies? Why do ladies get them?" Frances' worry grew, and she perspired.

The cook stared out the cafe's front window. He seemed to enjoy his cigarette, and the fact that Frances waited for his answer.

He said, "Folks get tumors when they take care a' other folk too much."

"What on earth do you mean?"

"Well, now, they's two reasons, actually. Lissen here: th' first reason is, when folks git so involved with their aunties, daddies, spouses, an' takin' care a' all their ol' grannies besides, not t' mention all th' babies an' what-not, it gits t' be too much, an' these folks get overloaded. B'cause, well, d'pendent relatives, see, they give off a kind a' germ."

"That can't be!" Frances was scarlet.

"Now, now; folks know this to be true. That germ makes folks have tumors! Now, the second reason folks get tumors is this: from soup."

"Soup! You don't serve soup here, do you?" she cried.

"Well, as a matter of fac', Missy, we do."

"Oh, no!" Frances turned away, hand pressed to her heart. "Yes, I've eaten soup here many times over the years. But how do you know all this? You're no scientist — you're a cook," she asserted.

The cook flicked away his cigarette and turned to the stove. " 'S'right. An' don' you ever ignore what a cook has t' say." He scowled darkly. "Now, did you see our waitress Corky run outta here?"

"She was crying."

"Yep. She got all riled up 'cause we run outta th' fruit juice she loves so. See, she's all sens'tive-like, 'cause she got tumors, an' takes care a' whole messa folks at home, 'course, includin' her ol' Granny, an' a baby whose teeth grew in real gray an' pointy. An' then there's all th' custormers she serves right here all day, as many as we git. All these people, they gave her th' germ, you kin be sure."

"So Corky has—a scar, like me?"

"Now, how would I know that, Frances?"

"But you just said—"

The cook breathed fiercely. "All right, sure, sure, she got a scar—she's chock-full a' scars, dammit, jus' like lots a' th' ladies, 'cept they's not scars we're talkin' 'bout, Frances, they's tumors."

"You're lying!"

"Suit yerself. Irregardless, you don' want t' be sittin' all alone in this world when them tumors inside you come bustin' out! See, I once had a friend, an' he was blind. An' he tol' me, 'It's th' mos' terrible thing in the world to be alone.' An' he knew this t' be a true fac' better'n you 'r me, b'cause he was blind."

"What are you talking about, Mal? There are no blind in Munson," she said.

The cook stamped out his cigarette, ducking a glance again through the pass-through and out the window. "Got an awful lot a' berries on th' trees this year."

Frances' mind tumbled with worry. She wanted to think about all the cook had said, including the news about soup, yet she was also worried about the hour.

Should she visit Nancy after all, even though night was setting in? Suddenly, she remembered something. "You're Mal—aren't you?" she asked the cook.

"Yep. We pick th' berries ourselfs, and make all kind a' recipe from 'em," the old man went on, tapping the spatula harder, with a clanging sound that struck Frances' nerves. "We get 'em before the lizards do, 'cause we pick at night. Right, Lucas?" He turned to the teenager on the crate beside him, who still ate from the cereal bowl.

Frances looked through the pass-through, too. "It's not a tumor," she went on quietly. "Palmer didn't say so. He said dozens of people get scars, and that these appear naturally, for no reason at all, exactly how a wart might suddenly appear, or the universe. So it's all very common, you see."

"Hmm. Tha's not th' way I heard it, Frances."

"Well, it doesn't matter to me, Mal! Because I'm leaving Munson."

"Heh! Fancy girl, 'ent you?"

Frances sighed, realizing she should not have mentioned her plan to Mal. She did not feel like arguing, either. Lifting and wiggling a sore ankle, then turning in the close, oil-smelling kitchen, another memory bolted through her. "I've been back here before, haven't I?"

"Dozens a' years ago, seems like. You were a cute child, Frances. What do y' do now?"

The sound of the man's voice, even the sight of his roughened, sinewy under-throat made her smile: long ago, in the diner's gravel parking lot, Mal had folded her up in his arms and pulled her to safety from her mother's parked car, which had been in the path of a telephone pole that fell and snarled the car with wires.

"I'm not sure yet what I'll do in life, but I think it's important to plan on something," she said.

Mal grinned faintly back to her. "How old are you, Frances?"

"Thirty-eight."

"Oh, well, then, y' got plenty a' time t' decide."

She took a long breath. "I'd like to work with animals someday, I think."

"Is tha' right?" The cook smiled rather arrogantly, then turned to the boy on the crate. "Lucas here worked at th' ol' slaughterhouse in Little-Munson, before he made a goddammned mess a' everything, that is." Lucas looked up and grinned, showing a thick row of slanting teeth, which he brought down hard on the spoon of mush.

"I liked my dog," Frances persisted tonelessly. "She was familiar to me! I don't like all animals. But there are so many of them—everywhere!"

The cook eyed her. "They is?"

"Animals live in the present, don't they, Mal? They don't worry about what's to come. They can forget bad things quickly! Is that a skill, or just a matter of luck? Why aren't we that way?"

"Oh, settle down," Mal grumbled. "You never know where an animal's been. Like a squirrel—they got an agenda, see, 'cause they's only thinkin' about themselfs."

"But Mal, that's how people are!"

"Heh!" the cook grinned saltily. "True."

"I miss my dog!" Frances cried then, explaining to Mal how Missie had rather slipped away into the bushes of the backyard, and an altogether wild existence.

"Yull never see that dog again!" Mal shook his head. "Look at yerself—all alone now, an' with that tumor!"

Frances dried her tears on the cord of an onion-bag. "Gosh, Mal, you're like all the others in this town—mean! Mean and small and always thinking of catastrophes."

"Naw, naw, I 'ent," he said, smoking again, blowing luxuriantly. "No, Frances, I'm jes' lookin' out fer you, is all. Y' don' understand Mal, now, do you?"

A wave of distaste rolled through her. Munson folks, as a group, were opaque and rambling; they were aggressive, too, and perhaps fearful. Am I as afraid of the unknown as they? Frances wondered, restlessly pinching fingertips along her skirt-hem. She could not determine it, nor did she know if it was the idea of leaving Munson that disturbed her, or virtually any decisive act at all. The thought of a long bus trip certainly made her nervous, yet so did the idea of eating in Mal's diner, with its possibility of bringing nausea or worse.

Would Frances Johnson find a way?

Mal extended a small key toward her face. ". . . It's from me t' you, Missy . . . so any ol' time, go on down there to th' cabin an' relax."

"You want me to use your forest cabin?"

"That's what I'm sayin', Frances! We don't use it anymore; I'm alt'gether too old. You use it! Go on out there. Get a ways outta town, so y' can rest."

"But your cabin isn't far out of town, Mal, not at all. It's one of those little cabins on the hill near the Hutchinson Dance Pavilion, isn't it?"

"Well, yep . . . but y' oughtta use it fer re-laxation, Frances. Why don't y' go there t' ferget about yer dog? They's a faucet there," he said, pushing the diminutive key into her hand.

"Well, all right, Mal—thanks," she said, puzzled,

pocketing the key.

He waved her away and began splitting nuts on the board while Frances turned to Lucas. Lucas' ears, she noticed, were stuffed with cotton, and he stared implacably at a rubber floor-mat. "What's wrong with him?" she asked, pointing to the cotton.

"Aw," Mal answered. "Don't bother with him. He gits scared plums'll grow in his ears, an' he means t' protec' 'em. I never mind th' boy comin' over here. D' y' know his mother, Frances? Clover's her name." Mal spat into a can.

Lucas and Clover were from Little-Munson, Frances recalled, looking at the boy uncomfortably. His large, wet lower incisors crowded out from his loose jaw as if seeking escape. He had an unappealing face, Frances decided, and in his chiding expressions, he seemed to know this and magnify the effect.

"How are you?" she asked the boy loudly.

Lucas' mouth was stained. "You're an orphan," he said in a silvery, musical voice. His eyes were angry and round.

"What did you say?"

"You don't have real parents." Lucas laughed, his crinkling eyes upon hers.

"Why does he say that?" Frances asked Mal nervously.

"I said don't mind him," Mal grumped.

"You're an adult orphan; it means you're alone, you have no one, and you'll just die," Lucas sang.

Frances gritted her teeth. "What are you talking about? I have parents."

"Nope. You're not part of them," he sang.

"And what about you?" she said to Lucas. "You're the one who probably doesn't have real parents. Why don't you wipe your mouth?"

Mal tinkered with two bare wires hanging in the stove's hood. "Shut up, boy," he said.

"My mother's young," Lucas sang on, lips thick and moist. "She's not perfect! But she knows me."

"Lucas's good with his hands," Mal remarked to Frances.

"You're not lucky!!" Lucas burst out, while Frances stared.

"I said don' mind him. He jes' likes t' tell all diff'rent kind a' tales," Mal observed, now upending a jar of olives onto a plate of crackers. "That's b'cause he's fanciful."

Frances moved away, pushing knuckles against the refrigerator door, now recalling, for some reason, her childhood home. One year, a tin-colored spot appeared at the end of her mother's shapeless brown sofa, seemingly without cause. This puzzled the family, and there was some speculation that the spot came from within the cushions themselves. Finally, the spot incited Frances' father to holler at her sister, accusing Valencia of a wrongful, lax association with a teenage boy who, the father said, had poor character and an unsuitable frame of mind. As it turned out, the father was right, because the next night the boy burned down a neighbor's shed. Then the Johnson family, except Valencia, all believed the boy had in fact caused the stain on one of his evening visits. But one weekend, with the aid of a flashlight and lemon juice, Frances' mother managed to prove this theory wrong. It was Frances who had caused the stain, she said, though Frances could not recall doing anything to stain the couch. For weeks she tried to recall the truth, but without success.

"... an' he didn't get any."

"What, Mal?"

"I said he doesn't care to be patted, or t' have any affections whatsoever." Lucas stared impassively ahead. "He usually keeps sep'rate-like from other folks. Well, it suits him. Do you like affection, Frances?" Mal asked.

"Oh, Mal, it's really not my style." She turned away, ready to leave, pulling a pill of flour off her shoe-sole.

Mal sniffed. "Corky's that way—real cold-like."

"Who said we're cold, Mal? We're not."

"It's darned odd. It 'ent nat'rul, among young folk."

"It is natural, Mal," she said wearily, "if that's how we are. Anyway, what about you? Don't you like affection?"

"I 'ent talkin' about me!" the cook bristled. "I'm talkin' about you, because I know all th' young people these days, an' I watched 'em fer years, an' I know yer not right in the mind, none of y'!" He violently scrubbed gristle-bits from the grill.

"Pfft!" Frances narrowed her eyes at him dismissively, then looked into the dining-room.

The cafe's bright light glowed into the parking lot and gravelly road beyond; there she saw what looked like a small hog maneuvering in the grass, stopping to lick something on the ground as patiently as would a cat. Frances' heart lurched, for the animal resembled Missie, at least around its rueful, lashy eyes. The hog glanced to the right, then left, its face feral and tender. The creature plunged into a thicket.

" 'Ent you goin' to the dance, Frances?"

She looked at Mal stoically. "The Munson dance? At the old pavilion where it floods rain enough to bring bloodworms onto the floor every year by the hundreds? I don't think so."

"Aw, Frances, y' oughtta go."

"Why should I? Ray's certainly busy that night, and I won't be going."

"With 'r without yer brother, Frances, y' should go. Why, all ladies do."

"Ray isn't my brother! Mal, why does everyone insist on believing he is? And why so much talk about the dance—have folks ever bothered to ask why the dance is supposedly so darned important?" A thin sheen of sweat sprang to her face, and Frances swiped at it impatiently.

Lucas whooped, laughing, eyes shining and rolling to the wall, and rhythmically he squeaked his fingertips along the rim of his cereal bowl.

Mal leaned forward intently, gripping Frances' arm with his own gray, ropy arm, breath smelling of bacon: "Dammit, girl, b'cause ev'ry dance is a crossroads! You know th' sayin': 'Go t' every dance y' can . . . ' Eh, I ferget th' last part a' th' sayin'. Y' know it, Lucas?"

"I never heard that saying or anything like it!" Frances yanked her arm away.

"You lissen here, Frances! Yull go t' th' dance, if y' know what's any good in this life at all!"

"'What's any good in life!?'" Her mouth pulled up in a sardonic smile. "Mal, for God's sake!"

"Don' y' hear me?" the man wheezed, nearly weepy now as he reached for a dirty towel. "It's—" He coughed into the towel. "—please go! 'Cause it's gonna be such a loada darned fun!"

"Mal, have you ever reminded yourself that formal dances are simply not the paradise you imagine?" Frances had a desire to fight the old man, even with her fists. "Don't you see that life is just not that way?"

"Which way, Frances? I'm jes' sayin', it's good to git out to th' dance ev'ry year, 'cause tha's what folks're supposed t' do!"

"My life isn't going to change because of one rotten dance. Mal, people lose their way so easily, and no dance can—"

"Now, gosh, here," the man said, grumbling, mouthing words to himself, reaching with a tremor to the highest metal shelf atop the grill, on which sat an enormous rusted corn can. "Here!" Mal said, plucking a key from atop the can. "Times 'ent so diff'rent than they ever was, Frances. They's good and they's bad in life, an' it 'ent good to stay home from th' dance! Take this, now; it's th' key t' my wife's dressin' shack. Ya know where th' place is—jes' next t' th' pavilion, near all th' other dressin' shacks, right where it's been all these years. Use th' shack, Frances! It'll help set y' right before you dance. Why, y' can put on all the fresh dresses y' need, epply makeup, try on shoes, an' all th' pretty, lacy things ladies love! Go on, take th' key!" Mal's voice wobbled, as if his heart had floated into his throat.

She stared in surprise. "Mal! The cabin first, and now your wife's dressing shack!? I don't understand!"

He waved her off. "Well, th' shacks're diff'rent—wee lil' rooms fer ladies to dress in, y'know, an' t' peek over t' th' dance floor an' see who's there. Why, that might be th' best fer you, Frances. B'sides, the shack is all private an' cozy-like, an'—"

Frances' face went dark. "You want me to bring men there, is that it, Mal? To the shack—or the cabin, or both!? Oh, first Kenny, and now you! Don't things around here ever change?" Her voice filled with tears.

"Now, don't git in a fix," Mal said.

"I have a boyfriend, Mal!"

"Well . . . see, he 'ent what seems right fer you, that fella. All folks think this. Now, some day yull meet a fella who'll charm y' t' death, one who'll take his place in town th' way a man oughtta, an' yull wonder what you were ever doin' in th' first place." Mal spoke softly. "Ray's a mite odd, Frances."

She nearly shrieked. "Just because he takes a lot of walks—! You don't know Ray! And you're just parroting what you heard in town, because you can't think for yourself or imagine that everyone else could ever be wrong! Oh, I tell you—"

Hand quaking, Mal wrenched the cabin key from Frances' smock pocket, and strung it, along with the shack key, onto a piece of dirty yarn, which he pressed back into her palm; then he shoved her entire arm against her chest. "Take both th' keys, Frances, jes' take 'em, and keep 'em! A dance kin change a girl, they say, an' . . . y' never know . . . y' might need both keys in a right hurry that day . . ." Mal seemed on the brink of some enormous disappointment, and touched his fingertips to his heart.

"Can't you be quiet about it? Oh, if it means so much to you, fine, I'll take the dumb keys! I won't use them, though."

"Heh! Y' will! Yull see—th' cabin's jes' grand, an' th' shack's a fine place fer dressin' up. They're both fine spots," he repeated vaguely.

Holding the keys, Frances stepped backward, bumping into a mop upended against the kitchen wall. Slowly, as if with the slowness of the town itself, the mop fell toward her, toward the floor, while Mal stood by, she noted, now with a peaceful expression on his face. Finally, the mop struck a tower of empty boxes that crashed down, racing across the floor. Frances ran from the kitchen.

※　　※　　※

The screen door made of soft, dirtied aluminum—into which were pressed images of herons and dozens of smaller birds—gave easily beneath Frances' touch. A slight kick or strike behind the door might distort the bird shapes, and already had, she noted. Yellowish light from the porch's bulb slicked the windows, the wooden stair and a portion of the grass; beyond, inky, intractable night saturated the street. As Munson's council had never much cared for erecting street-lamps, the town was known for its nights of profound, mineral darkness. Some quality in the darkness always led Frances—and most townsfolk—into a near-helpless, paralytic grogginess each evening after supper, a sleepiness that was delicious in one way, yet also unpleasant because of its power. The grogginess led to ferociously deep sleep for most, though for Frances, the relief of sleep was more elusive.

At the same time sleep brought rest, it brought the possibility of predation, she knew. For that reason, Frances often struggled against her evening grogginess, even though she desired sleep. In the end, she took the pills to help.

She leaned now against the porch beam, blinking,

a soft expression on her face. The cool air was loaded with fog droplets. Frances' eyes settled on some small, calcareous-looking objects in the dark yard: a hose, an empty flower-pot she employed as a spade, a dwarf tree with its surrounding fallen fruit. Frances wondered if her Munson ancestors had known the same irresistible sleepiness, and if they, like she, struggled with it over the years. In the distance she made out the window of the local hair salon, and beyond that, the hunkered-down shape of the high school gym.

A number of birds or bats swept past her face with astonishing speed, landing beneath the eaves. Frances felt alone. She pressed a dense, ferrous taste from her tongue, glancing at the porch swing, then at her fingers, recalling an evening much like this one when, as a teen, solitary as now, she had rubbed her palms down her hips as if to prime herself for the future, believing her life would embody, beginning that moment, a single, understandable story. But this idea had been wrong. "I have no frame," she spoke loudly to no one in the tranquilizing dark, thinking how, tonight, she would flip her body to one side of the bed, then the other, until she dropped to sleep from exhaustion or pills. Frances suspected that she even fought herself physically during sleep, but she was not sure. In brief, slashing glimpses, she recalled sensations of nighttime fury.

Frances did not care for the idea that her life should have an overall guiding structure, or frame. Yet she wanted one.

What kind of woman could Frances Johnson be or avoid being?

Remaining at the porch beam, she anticipated the limp,

thin sheet of her bed and its propensity to twist into a spiral. Frances wished to call someone, but it was unduly, extravagantly late, too late to use the telephone, anyway. And whom to call? Perhaps someone she had forgotten, a type of friend, a blank to be filled in, not her mother.

Frances heard a noise in the yard. It was Ray, carrying a bucket. He steered around the gutter pipe in the dark, then poured rippleless water from the bucket onto the lowest porch step. "I dug up that vine growing on the fence today," he told her. Ray did not care for vigorous plant life.

He tied a rope around the neck of a soft white sack that contained the dead vine, presumably, and other refuse.

Ray stood on the porch, facing her, posture solid and tall. "Frances," he remarked, "I want your life to be fruitful, not only for yourself, but for others."

"Oh, make sense, Ray," she said irritably.

"Someone wants to meet you," he said. "Mark."

Her temper flared at the prospect of another introduction. "God!" she cried. "Mark Hodgkins? For the love of Hell, why?" Mark Hodgkins owned Munson's cinema. The place was perpetually damp from its old carpeting, which, patterned in violent green whorls, always retained moisture from springtime rains. Hodgkins had worked hard through the years to dry the carpet, installing numbers of electric fans throughout the theater, each larger than the next, but to no avail; the place remained dank as it had been on the day Hodgkins purchased the building and planned it to be a bright entertainment-spot for the town.

Though the cinema did not succeed in the way he wished, Hodgkins' efforts were still impressive, because he was a man who had trouble moving the bones in his fingers, jaw, arms, and legs due to a creeping, indeterminate illness. As Frances' father had once remarked, Mark Hodgkins had compensated beautifully for his bad luck in one of life's biggest areas—the body. Hodgkins was not a gloomy man. He often joked, and carried colorful magazines in his coat pocket.

"I already know Hodgkins, don't you realize that?" Frances told Ray, sighing angrily. "And dammit, Ray, it's getting late!"

"No, Frances. Not Mark Hodgkins."

"Well, who then, Ray?"

"I'm talking about Doctor Mark Carol."

The sound of the unfamiliar name rang jaggedly into the dark. It was unusual to hear an unknown name in Munson, and this one stopped Frances with a sting as brief as the name itself. A weight in Ray's voice caused her to feel that the strange man was inevitable, and that the uttering of his name made him part of her.

"Mark Carol?"

"Yes," said Ray.

"Are you sure you don't mean Mark Hodgkins?" she asked with dying hope.

From the side of the house a man appeared, hand extended toward Frances as he climbed the steps; she gripped her skirt and did not shake his hand. The stranger's face swelled into a smile. "Hallo! I'm new here, but of course you know that. I came to Munson just yesterday to practice medicine, and practice I will, if you-all will have me, that is. And I hope you will."

"We already have a doctor in this town!" Frances yelled wildly.

Mark Carol stepped closer.

He was an attractive man with a large, tanned, healthful face and a big chin-dimple. Although the regularity of his features worked to calm Frances slightly, the man's ears were extraordinarily large and somewhat cone-shaped, almost, she noticed, like miniature hats. She found his handsomeness enjoyable, though, and with this, she writhed uncomfortably. Martin French crossed her mind, as did other men who had visited Munson.

Mark Carol's eyes glinted with a smile. "Ah. Don't worry; sometimes when folks say they don't want a new doctor, it's often the case that they actually do need one!" He laughed.

Ray picked up the bucket gently, swaying it.

"I'll be frank," Carol told them. "California was not for me, so I left. My great-aunt lives here in town—Heidi."

"Ah, Heidi," Frances and Ray said at once, softly. The aunt was a weak, older woman who lived atop a butte.

"We still don't need another doctor!" Frances exploded, and Mark Carol gave a quiet chuckle, glancing at Ray. "That's an honest reaction, Frances, and I appreciate it thoroughly!"

Frances noticed a peculiar fog stealing across the nighttime yard. It was a fog of dull color, not characterized by a whitish contrast to darkness, but instead by a similarity to it—a brown, obscuring fog. Without hesitation, it rose around the house and porch and touched her; she backed away, watching the two men. The fog was granular like sand. Frances reached quickly as if to hold something, for example, a type of metal handle. The night seemed to change, and the bitter-tasting fog was everywhere.

Ray waded into the recesses of the lawn, a small sea in

which he was a purple shadow. She ran to him. "What do you mean by introducing me to this man?" she rasped.

"It wasn't my idea!" he whispered. "Frances . . . everyone in town wants you to begin your life in earnest; we both know it's true! Oh, Frances," he said with uncharacteristic emotion, "I just can't compete!" He receded quickly to the rear yard with its shed, swinging the bucket behind him.

Mark Carol gently tapped her from behind. "By the way, I met your mother tonight, and boy, is she a pip!"

She felt herself turn red. "You met my mother? Where?"

"At the bakery," the man said easily. "They kept the place open late tonight, because a muskrat got in. In all the commotion, she and I stepped outside with warm mugs of coffee and had a long chat." He laughed, patting his thigh.

Frances ran her eyes along the smiling doctor's lean, tanned neck and arms, then bolted inside the house and into her bed. After a long period of silence during which she waited, ears attuned, she heard a creaking step or two, then voices. A door whined: Ray and Mark Carol were descending the basement stairs.

"Frances!" Ray called out. "I'm going to show Doctor Carol my game-room!" She thought his voice sounded tense, but could not be sure. Did Ray really seek Carol's friendship? Frances was too troubled to know. The men's grit-sounding shoe steps echoed down the stair cavity, Ray's voice still audible: "Did you know the average career of a Red Baron pilot was only two weeks?"

Closing her eyes to put the fog at bay, wrapping herself in the sheet, she imagined Ray and the doctor playing board-games or re-creating a battle scene, possibly Verdun. After some time, her body softened into the narrow bed; Frances suspected she would rise the next morning to clean the downstairs game-table of a litter of glue, popsicle sticks, drink cups, and other traces of the men's evening together, but she would not be able to discern the character of that time, nor the degree of suspicion between the men, nor why, in fact, the doctor's presence jolted her so.

Frances swam in the sheet. Now, the components of night spread as if possessing a rolling mass, and, as if the mass contained her, too, Frances pushed upward, struggling against the town's grogginess, fog, and spark-like angers that burst for brief moments in her mind as if upon Munson's wide horizon. A longing arose for her sister who had departed years ago, and for Missie, as did a powerful wish for radishes; she listened outside to a screech of some unknown critter hurtling across the neighborhood yards.

Then, unable to stop herself, Frances deeply imagined the kiss of Doctor Mark Carol, which would have its own texture and taste like chalk or lima beans. As she turned in the bed, Munson's pressures and demands were upon her as well, powerful as squeezing fists. "But I am Munson!" she cried, giggling too because it was true. She felt folks rustling very close, glum, and whispering inside her; Doctor Carol's eyes smiled amongst them, no different from her eyes at all. It frightened Frances. She was not herself with all Munson's voices inside her, and not herself without them, either. She thought sadly of the many shoe-and-skirt sets purchased downtown, and how difficult it would be to depart for good, leaving these behind.

Sleeping, she quickly dreamed herself wandering near a beveled wall in a restaurant not unlike Ming's tavern, dark and empty. She lay motionless atop a bright orange platform of churning machinery that roared beside her, and she watched oily gears turning larger gears.

She woke in the bed, lost. It was true, perhaps: she must begin her life, but in what way? Doctor Carol's pearly face appeared again in her mind and she pulsed, lowering herself to the mattress again with a strongly sensual movement, sleeping and waking repeatedly.

A bright light often precedes the blasting sound of an explosion, Frances reflected, lying there. Or did it? Perhaps as a blast pierces the sky, it must carve a crack, a tunnel in air through which to express its light, given that light must be sent away somewhere, she reasoned. She woke fully now and rose from the bed, grabbing one of the unraveling sweaters from her chair, hurrying through the house. The front yard was saturated with blossoms' fragrances, and the difficult brown fog was gone. Frances' bicycle glistened with early dew, propped against a young tree. She rode fast, toward town.

*   *   *

The roads were uncharacteristically dusty and sweet-smelling as Frances' bicycle wheels swirled through the dirt, bumping and skidding. She would find Nancy's house as soon as possible, despite her previous failure to do so. Half-sliding down a weedy slope where no one ever walked, she grinned at her own clear-sightedness in finding this simple and time-saving shortcut. The bike skirted an oval concrete rim around a small, unpopular park that was also a sore point with many locals, for the men who built the park had forgotten to consult the town council or sheriffs about it. The park stood in extreme proximity to a group of Little-Munson's dusty back-streets. This bothered many folks, and some Munson residents shunned the park, saying it was an eyesore. It was true that the park was drab, and its stone drinking fountain was busy with beetles that would not leave. Recently, the town decided to close the park, and a metal fence would surround it soon.

Between dark and diagonal streets, she saw what looked like a wild mule grazing calmly; Frances looked away, fearful the animal would remind her of Missie.

Then, at a distance, she saw Palmer, striding ahead past an abandoned sandwich shop.

She called out.

"Hallo Frances!" he cried back. "I thought about you earlier!"

She stepped astride the bicycle. A tree hovered over the old shop and its porch lamp, and bright green, featherlike seeds spilled from the branches, breaking into smaller, greener seeds that floated lightly to the porch, collecting into an anvil-shaped mass with a sodden edge.

"I'm en route to see Nancy. But Palmer, don't tell her—or anyone!—that I want to leave Munson. Please? Because I'm not sure I'll be able to manage the trip." She took his elbow comfortably. "Folks will be upset if they find out I want to leave."

"Sure," he said cheerfully. Palmer went on, exclaiming softly, "It's strange! Tonight I tuned into the radio, and heard a tale about a diseased boy living in another state. He's a very poor boy, Frances. Do you know that men in a hospital removed his heart and gave him a rubber one? How marvelous, I thought! That boy is part of a new world. After all that, is he still a mere boy? I don't know! Will he be required to accept the horrors and dilemmas of the new world? You bet. But I envy him, Frances. Maybe he'll never die."

She listened, slightly awed.

"Do you know what else?" he asked.

"What?"

"Yesterday—was the first time you and I have really spoken, Frances."

"Oh, I know. I—"

"You hardly spoke last year. You were silent as, as a tomato. When did you learn to hold your own?"

A sleek wind slipped around the porch landing, carrying a hint of a whistle, throwing Frances' hair against her cheek. She felt as if the admiring man might touch the hair. "Recently."

"Ha!" He shouted to the empty street. "Well, dandy. It's as if you've just awakened from a long, deep sleep! In my eyes, of course."

She laughed with a honking sound that startled the older man. "And I used to think you were evil!" He grinned deeply, baring the small teeth. Then, astonished, she saw the man's eyes grow rimfuls of tears.

She sat beside him on the crumbling stoop of the old sandwich shop amidst the soft, feathery tree-seeds. "Palmer, someone new has arrived in town, and it's a doctor!"

"Heh?"

"I met him—his name is Mark Carol."

"Oh! Is he bossy?"

"I think so. And he's been on my mind in a terrible way. I just don't trust him."

The doctor nodded. "I'd pay attention to that feeling," he said.

Frances leaned her elbow thoughtfully toward her knee and missed, so that her shoulder and head crashed uncontrollably for a moment upon her leg.

"Say," the man said, "do you ever feel shame? I do."

She rubbed an eye-tooth. "Shame about what?"

"Oh, about nearly every darned thing."

Frances remarked, "You are so open!"

He nodded. "I feel less shame nowadays than in my youth, when I lived in California—it's a greedy, terrible state. In it, I was greedy too."

"In what way?"

". . . Frances, people want so much, all the time. Why is that?"

"Animals don't want much, Palmer."

"The hell they don't! Now listen—Mark Carol conjures up all these thoughts, for me."

"You mean you know Mark Carol?" For a second time Frances was astonished.

"I do. He and I studied at the same coastal medical school. We were friends, even had the same eyes and coloring, some said. In those days, you see, I was part of a young generation in which I, Mark Carol, and several ladies present quickly became the center of a group that questioned our world and its ideas. Then something else developed. Every afternoon, Carol and I sat on the benches of the dairy bar, each man flipping his textbook pages faster, faster, in a race to know more! Then the competition grew uglier than that. Not unprovoked, Carol tried to discredit me in front of the whole class!"

"Why, Palmer?"

"Because I had musical leanings, among other things. You see, sometimes I tried to shield myself from the world by living inside a song."

"That's strange."

"Not really—or in that time and place, it wasn't. Oh, I would listen to one piece of music over and over—I still love the sound of a lone oboe along with a little tambourine. Well, one day in class, Carol called me names. He said I would never make a doctor, but that he would. That made me mad!"

"And you're still mad?" she asked.

"No, Frances, not really. I'm more of a regretter. Carol and I never resolved our dreadful competition, and I behaved badly."

"Perhaps you both behaved badly, Palmer."

"Ha! I fled California years ago, not only because of Carol, but for other reasons having to do with a stolen zither. Regret and shame are hard masters," he added rather haplessly. "And now, Mark Carol has come here, to Munson? Life is weird, Frances."

"His aunt is Heidi."

"Ah, Heidi," said the doctor, touching his palms together. "Her feet cause her to suffer. —Frances, your impulse to leave Munson is correct. Leave! It's the site of your dreams, and the site of dreams should always be left behind."

She understood only vaguely. "Palmer, do you have a wife?"

"I don't know!"

"Well," she paused— "neither do I have an official

mate, but there are people here—all over town, Palmer—who want me to behave in accordance with their wishes, just as would a bitter, controlling spouse."

"Which people?"

She gestured. "Oh, Palmer! Don't you feel it? It's the way folks stare from their windows and whisper to each other on the street. The pressure in the atmosphere—it's everywhere! What, Palmer?" she asked, for the doctor was digging fiercely into his ear with a finger.

He stopped, looking at her. "I can't say that I feel it. But I believe you, Frances, and can guess how, as a young person, you might feel. Why have you stayed in Munson this long? Go someplace new," he said, "and begin again."

"That's what you did, Palmer."

"Oh!" he said, eyes filling, as if he had not realized it.

The man scooted forward. "Frances, what if I were to ask you to help me with an errand?"

"Errand? What errand?"

"I'm no competer," Palmer began with controlled excitement. "But like most professionals, I've long been drawing up elaborate plans in my bedroom at night. I may have mentioned my experiments before . . . you see, I've been tinkering with a wax-and-oil compound for quite a while. The project excites me terribly, Frances. To be exact, I'm trying to invent a special balm."

She listened with absorption, watching the man's chin and its movements.

"I hope that one day, this balm will stand up to criticism, and maybe even help people far away. Does that sound silly?" The man stared ahead, pushing his glasses up his nose, resting his forearms on lean knees. "Well, you see, there's a particular ingredient I need to finish the project, but lack. The stuff isn't available in Munson—"

"You're not like anyone," she observed.

"...and which is not exotic, by any means. It is, however, an unusual, semihardened oil with some far-reaching, healthful properties I've long admired. I want my balm to have pizzazz! Searching for far-flung ingredients is not my forte, however, and I can't take time to travel, not with my responsibilities in town. Frances—can you help? If you find the oil for me, I think it would help us both. Besides, travel makes me queasy. I need the darned oil—"

"What sort of oil?"

"Chicken-beak oil," he replied, "and lots of it. Can the stuff be found in this state? Christ, no! You have to look elsewhere," he added softly, and his light eyes bored into hers. "This errand could help you leave town, Frances, as a push, a starting point, a way out of your own hesitation. If you go, I'll be standing right behind you."

She scuffed her shoe on the stoop. "How would the errand help me leave Munson for good? I haven't faith in that, Palmer. I've never been able to leave before."

"Ah, Frances—then you must stand atop a crest of your own creation, and ask yourself, 'What makes this moment different from previous moments?' And have courage. After you cross the state line, find the oil, purchase it, then mail it to me, you'll be a new woman, I bet."

She thumbed the toe of her shoe gently as she and the man breathed the night silence.

"Will this balm of yours put you ahead of Mark Carol?" she asked.

"Ah. As I say, Frances, I'm no competer, not anymore. I'm a dweller. I dwell on the things that intrigue me." He bent his head and exhaled, his breath scented of a sweet drink, perhaps grape juice. "What I'm after," he said, "I can't exactly explain. The excitement of a new endeavor, maybe. Or the way time passes so happily while I'm working on the balm. But—I feel guilty, Frances," he breathed. "Is it wrong to invent new things that aren't absolutely necessary to life?"

" 'Course not," she answered firmly.

"Then—will you help me find some of that oil?" Palmer's long face was damp and flushed, and she keenly sensed the newness of their friendship, which had begun, in fact, only hours before. She grinned awkwardly, bumping her knees together hard.

"Once you find the stuff, you can just send it to me in a series of pipettes. I trust you, Frances," the doctor said shyly, "and I'll pack you a dropper." He waited then, blinking; beside them on the step, the mass of tree-seeds spilled upward into a gust of wind, and it occurred to Frances that the man might have no other friends.

"Well, I could try," she offered.

"Ha-ha!" Palmer shouted, slapping a leg. "This is tremendous. Don't neglect your health on this journey, now, Frances. Take a hairbrush along. Oh, don't underestimate the power of this oil. It could bring us both an enormous font of good. Can you leave soon?"

She cried out abruptly, "Palmer, what about the scar? How can I travel with it—what if it grows worse, and I have to go to a hospital?"

He bellowed with fierce annoyance, standing, "You won't have to go to a hospital!" then strode away on lanky legs. At some distance he turned. "Don't you see? The scar is—well, tantamount to nothing."

Dumbfounded, she stared. Then Frances turned away, breathing dreamily, having rather enjoyed the man's flash of temper. Moving to the ledge of the sidewalk, rising to her toes, she sensed her skirt lift in the evening breeze, glad for the news about the scar, while a sudden appreciation of power—of the impulse to take and take, to win and win—stole through her body excitingly. Palmer had disappeared into the bluish dark of the street; smiling, tipping her head back, feeling herself impervious, she regarded the street-lamp, with its wavering, refracted colors, through slitted eyelids. Another Frances Johnson existed somewhere, she saw from her tip-toes: a lighter person who rode along life as if upon scallopy air currents complex as fortune itself. The other Frances looked different, had different precepts and a different bodily carriage; she was a woman who was not a woman and lived in a place as spacious and rare as a moon.

Frances rode along the bank of a lake so finely reflective that it was much more than a lake, though freckled by gnats and transparent fish; when she opened her eyes to touch the lake's surface, she saw herself beneath it, surprised, breath held tight in full, rounded cheeks.

*   *   *

Frances pedaled along the road. She wanted to embrace someone, though she could not imagine who. Clothing formed a shield, and embraces were unsatisfying, in any case, because they pointed toward an end of achieving a goal and nothing more. Frances' eyes felt hot. The bicycle spun atop layers of the thick green seeds, then rolled faster, as if in special collusion with gravity, bumping quickly away from the lake. Vaguely contented with the whirring bike, she crossed railroad tracks that had fallen into disuse, half-buried in soot, then raced into an open, immense field of yellow straw that extended in all directions, dwarfing her. Pedaling harder, she saw the low, free-standing buildings that comprised the town bakery where Happy Jaine had worked long ago. The bakery produced crackers and other edibles for the town; its owner, Mrs. Mars, was a stout woman who moved slowly and with certainty and sometimes liked to test her crackers' crispness with a dowel. Overall, Mrs. Mars once had said, she disliked baking and bakers, but through the years, she grew attached to business and its porous routines, and decided to keep the bakery until she died.

Once, years before, Mrs. Mars rather abruptly had asked Frances' mother in the bakery with its sweat-laden windows, "Isn't there some way to forget the past?" And Frances' mother had quipped, "What about forgetting the present?" then searched through her dark purse. Mrs. Mars, patting sadly at her own breast, said it was fortunate that the present existed at all, because it could be used as a barrier to the past; but Frances' mother, who generally did not like to talk about such things, grabbed Frances' hand and ran from the shop.

Long ago, Mrs. Mars had twins; then she had twins again. Now, the four twins, adult men and women all, were large, busy people, often in a hurry, eyes to the ground. The four of them worked hard in Munson, all putting in long hours at a shop specializing in paper and nuts. The twins' mouths went in long, straight lines, which, Frances' aunt once had remarked in a rustling whisper, formed a trail leading straight back to the bakery where they had been born. No one knew what the twins ever thought, since they were extremely polite, always quiet and busy, their personalities recessive. Folks knew that Mrs. Mars was puzzled by her brood, and for years had sometimes cried into a napkin at night because she was terribly hurt that her twins were different, and even looked different, perhaps fleshier and lunkier, than other children.

Later in her life, Mrs. Mars had another relative living with her, a brother or cousin who, folks said, was different yet again from other children. The relative's name was Ray, just like Ray Garn, but whereas Frances' Ray was generally civil, Ray Mars was trouble. From a young age, Ray Mars had been considered rude, and as a younger boy, he behaved like an older teen, yelling, smoking, roughhousing, or diving into shrubbery. Once, he buttered Mrs. Mars' sofa so that she was unable to use it or ask anyone to sit on it at all, so that Mrs. Mars had to call some men to come haul the sofa away, and she grew angry.

When in high school, Ray Mars was recognizable for his longish hair and gangly limbs. Loudly and often, he proclaimed in public that he wanted another family, which upset townsfolk to hear, and one summer, he yelled such a statement inside the bakery door. Ray Mars was genuinely upset, so Mrs. Mars rose from her stool and took the propping-stick from the bakery window, which sluggishly fell shut, and the sound of Ray Mars' voice could not get in.

He stole emery boards and other sundries from the local drugstore, and when the Munson sheriffs pressed him for answers, Ray Mars told them that he deserved those things, and the sheriffs laughed, asking him what else he thought he deserved.

"I deserve everything! Everything everyone else has and more!" Ray Mars screamed, and the men laughed harder. One sheriff held a white lizard and put it on Ray Mars' shoulder, making the teenager thrash his arms and upset his chair in sudden fear. It seemed the men enjoyed Ray Mars because he was a teen, and so was hard to reach and attractively weak; the men bothered and prodded him as much as they could. Some years later, Frances heard that Ray Mars had grown extremely unkempt, and spent most of his time in the woods.

When she was twenty-one and living again at her parents' home, Frances went one afternoon to the far end of her mother's street, Sarah Lane, rooting for lost car parts. Far inside the shrubs, at a hillside, she found a small cave entrance. Frances had heard of a cave near the end of Sarah Lane, but always thought it was make-believe; now she knew otherwise, and was curious. Scooting inside the hole, she shrieked, for she thought she saw three bats crawling in a circle. But it was merely an old can of peas with a torn label; looking up the rock passage then, Frances knew, as if some prognostic voice told her so, that a man lived in this cave, and that it was Ray Mars.

Stooping, she proceeded along a ledge with the placidity sometimes native to her nature, and peering into the cave, she smiled to see that it was comfortably furnished. She saw, too, that Ray Mars was not dirty, but, to the contrary, was a handsome, well-groomed man who stored his clothes neatly on a rock.

"Hello," he said.

Frances stayed that afternoon in the cave, listening to

original guitar compositions the young man played for her as they lounged on an orange carpet, with Ray Mars ultimately kissing Frances' lips fully for a long minute after his musical playing. During the kiss, her innards rose to her throat, and she opened her eyes to the cave ceiling where numerous guitars hung from metal hooks and coiled wires, for Ray Mars owned these guitars, and he stored them in this way.

Ray Mars was older than she thought, older than anyone from her former class, maybe, and his eyes, the color of lake water, were skittish. His facial skin was scarred and tight, and Frances saw uncomfortably how the town did not trust Ray Mars, with the skin possibly a contributing factor to this, although it should not have been so. And suddenly she had the urge to defy the townsfolk and become the lover of Ray Mars, except that, looking at the heavily breathing man, Frances wanted most of all to go home.

Ray Mars lay back, looking to the guitars on the ceiling, too. Then he said, "Frances, you probably don't know that I've taken another name. I'm not Ray anymore."

"You're not?" she asked, not understanding, portraying a sophisticated amusement. "Who are you, then?"

"Stinky."

"Stinky?" she blurted, surprised. "Stinky Mars?"

"That's right," he said self-consciously. "It's a tough-sounding name, a lot of folks say."

Frances giggled into her paper cone of water, and asked him what it meant.

His eyes turned furious and Ray Mars hollered, "It doesn't mean a damned thing!" and Frances looked to her knees.

"Well," the young man added more softly, "it's actually a long story. But still, you needn't call me Ray anymore."

"Why not?"

"Because I've changed. I'm all different," he said importantly, looking around the cave with its guitars and stacks of batteries and sponges in barrels. "If you want to know the truth . . . Do you?"

"Yes."

"All right. You probably know I always wanted a whole new family. Well, I found one!"

"You did?"

"Yes, and they are terrific!"

"Who are they? And where are they?" she asked eagerly.

"See," he explained, "they're real busy right now. They're away and won't be back for a long time, but they like me a lot, and their name for me is 'Stinky.' "

"Why on earth do they call you that?"

"Because, dope, it's an endearment! Haven't you ever heard of that?"

Frances said she had.

"The family does all sorts of things, like play games and give presents. They took me to dinner at Mal's at least ten times. My new family is great. It's just that right now, they're away. I don't even think about my old family anymore."

Frances was puzzled, but happy for Ray Mars, and with some delight she laughed, perhaps too loudly, for Ray Mars pushed himself back into the corner and began to whittle.

For all her discomfort with the kiss, Frances enjoyed

being in the cave with Ray Mars, away from home and independent. Time passed then in a quick, glittering downrush, as if it had reconnoitered and found its true course there in the cave with the mini-refrigerator and the promise of Ray Mars' new family. She tasted something as warm and indescribable as an abruptly opened vein of memory, and recalled the metallic scent of rain upon the high school's roof during the years she sat listlessly in classrooms beside her classmates, always waiting for something else. Frances did not know how long she sat in silence with Ray Mars in the cave; outside, at a distance, she heard a car sliding past.

Suddenly she recalled the musty odor of her parents' home, and the even sweeter perfusion of her own slanted bed. "I must leave," she told the man frantically, and staggered to her feet.

As he waved her goodbye, he gave a mild grin, saying his phone number would be changed the following day. He handed Frances some crackers. Running lightly on her toes, the dirt of the path cool and vivid, she was so relieved to be fully alone that she wondered if she had been attacked. No, she had not been, she thought. But what constituted attack? The mush of the woods' decomposed leaves clung to her shoes like treacle, and Frances swore she would not tell anyone about the afternoon with Ray Mars: her sister would scoff about it, in any case, and say she lacked discernment.

Frances could not sleep that night. The events of the day swelled in her mind, pitching inside her with the lawlessness of anger. She felt no anchor, and finally slipped from her bed to summon her mother from the roof.

She described the afternoon's events to her mother

as the thin woman sat rocking on the edge of the bed. "God, what a fiasco!" her mother groaned painfully, grabbing her arms around herself, saying it was terrible that Frances must now bear the ignominy of having been kissed without having received a gift.

Frances waited, then suddenly cried, holding the packet high in the air, "But Mother, wait! He did give me something: crackers!"

"Shut the hell up!" the mother fumed, running down the dark hall. Her mother informed her then, whirling through the rooms in her flowered house-dress, moaning, that Ray Mars and his dwelling-place were filthy nearly to the point of being excretory, that he would certainly harm Frances or already had, and then she ran outside, shouting from the back lawn that they were going to see the doctor on the next business day.

From that point until the moment she faced the old doctor and allowed him to examine her, Frances sank into a stupor of sickish discomfort, unable to eat or sleep, just as her mother predicted would happen. Splinters of images from the afternoon in the cave erupted in her mind: Ray Mars' yellowish, scarred face, his split fingernails and teeth, the guitars hanging above with their curling strings—each image brought her further into the depthless sickness.

After the doctor's appointment, she walked into the warm sun on Munson's main street, feeling vaguely relieved; masses of birds hung in the elder trees. Her mother came to Frances, taking her limp hand, and together they went to the end of Sarah Lane.

Frances' mother stooped near the entrance of the cave while Frances stood behind her, squinting torpidly into the sun. "Yoo-hoo!" her mother shouted into the lair, and Frances heard Ray Mars' muffled voice. The brief, quiet exchange that ensued between the man and the mother, garbled as the nonsense sound of water falling into a bathtub, numbed Frances further. Waiting there, she grew aware of a vast force that existed everywhere: bigger than any town, flexible and invisible, it could squeeze the world as it desired, leaving nothing untouched.

Her mother stood upright, flinging a fist that looked uncannily like a small, frantic head, yelling into Ray Mars' cave, "If I ever see you near Frances again, I'll beat the crap out of you!" And the mother and daughter went home.

*   *   *

Frances rode on that morning. A pleasant numbness spread through her bottom, a response to the road's numerous hard, irregular bumps and dirt-mounds that transmitted sharply through the bicycle frame to her bones. Despite her previous concerns, now she was sure that a visit to Nancy would be real. In minutes she would arrive at Nancy's house, and Nancy would be inside; the day would fall open like a gentle plume. Together, she and Nancy would joke, enjoying themselves for hours.

Frances did not know why, but it seemed she and Nancy had always been racing toward a horizon together, and at the race's end, each woman would stop suddenly, realizing she had lost sight of the other for good. The final moment of their friendship would be abrupt, she thought, and would contain so much distended regret that it would need to be siphoned away, as if through a pipeline to the open sea.

Frances now was able to recall her last visit to Nancy; it had been on a rainy day during which she had lain on the woman's sofa, feeling the hapless, mealy pleasure that arises from the absence of pain, for on that day, a long-standing headache had vanished. Nancy had worn, instead of her usual straight skirt, a pair of pink pajamas. The sky that day had a light, cottony aspect, with low-tumbling clouds propelled forward by wind gusts that lifted both women's hair nearly straight above their heads as they hiked around the house and yard, Nancy pulling a tweed coat tightly over her robe. She had wanted to show Frances her new car, but complained that the vehicle was too tall and lacked elbow room; Frances disagreed, and quite liked the enormous vehicle, which was upright and formal as an old-fashioned, elegant carriage. Nancy said the car weighed eight tons. She opened its door and stuck her head inside.

"Dammit," she cursed, "it's dark in here! Yesterday I needed some papers in the back seat, but I couldn't see a thing . . . when I reached in, I felt something so terrible and squishy!"

"My gosh, Nancy! What was it?"

"A raisin!"

Later, for warmth, Nancy made the scalding, smoky-black coffee that Frances often enjoyed, the drink's burnt taste and uncompromising bitterness releasing a mélange of unmitigated flavors on her tongue, working to calm her. A hundred questions arose then in her mind for Nancy alone, though Frances did not utter them. Instead, she waited while the drink's properties spread through her, a refraction of salts, sands, and minerals so expansive that it was rather miraculous to taste them there, Frances thought, in Nancy's cramped, green kitchen.

Now, in the early morning haze, she leaned her bicycle in front of the woman's house, craving the hot coffee and its charred scent. She stood motionless in the cold air of the yard, facing Nancy's door, waiting for full sun and Nancy, water seeping through her hard shoes; she climbed the front stairs. Presently she withdrew the key to her own house from her smock pocket, and, stepping across the porch, tried it uncertainly in the lock. The door fell open, and, smiling, Frances passed through the kitchen and into the living-room with its yellow centerpiece of a sofa, waiting there for an hour until the sun began to blaze through the bare windows. Then Nancy was standing at the bottom of the staircase, wearing a blue dirndl.

"Hallo," the woman said, strolling through the room, limbs swinging loosely, carelessly.

Frances often marveled at Nancy's physique, both plump and willowy-tall at once. The woman's intrepid glances were, though sometimes piercing and hard to bear, always satisfyingly attentive. Yet townsfolk who knew Nancy always spoke with hesitation about her. As they often remarked, she was born in the city of New York. Why was she in Munson now? No one knew, and no one seemed to remember how or when, or to what purpose, on a day long ago, Nancy had slipped into town. Her remote house, its edifice nearly eaten away by the snaking ivy, was still lovelier than any dwelling in Munson, and perhaps for this reason folks bore her grudges.

Nancy did not seem to care. Small, superb lights glinted white in her home's upper windows at night, and a heavy-leafed tree drooped in her side yard, its odorous blossoms often blowing through a window into Nancy's bathtub. Clinging to Nancy's fingers were many bright, heavy rings. At times, Frances believed the older woman nearly to be a type of queen.

Nancy wandered into another room, then back; she sat opposite Frances, who stared at her wordlessly. Nancy's age was difficult to determine. Her air was one of pleasant self-containment, though right now, she repeatedly thrust a hand into an empty can sitting on an end-table, fishing for crackers that weren't there. The conversation began fitfully, and Nancy stuck a thick cigarette in her mouth, which Frances realized might have been a type of cigar. Nancy did not light it.

The room's rear window faced a dune, and Frances watched a small woodpecker in the sand. "Is anyone allowed on that beach nowadays?" Frances asked with the flat, inquisitive air of a child.

"You know the town doesn't permit it," Nancy answered calmly. "Too dangerous, or so they say." Then she recalled, "Frances, you recently told me you had several dreams about chopped onions," and Frances nodded rhythmically, smiling happily as the two women found the thread of a familiar, meandering dialogue that proceeded in the halting yet serene manner of a snail crossing a road over hours, unaware of time; and forgetting the time indeed, not interested in turning back, the friends talked, less in a conversation with a point than in a kind of unstoppable practice that neither woman wished to end.

Frances was unmindful of the odor of school paste in the room, and during the course of their talk, Nancy asked Frances a few questions, including one about the word "contentment": whether it implied, to Frances, a fleeting sensation, or a long-term condition.

"Contentment—it's always a brief feeling, these days, isn't it?" Frances replied, and then she asked Nancy about acne. "Is it passed down through generations, do you think?"

"Well, fears certainly may be passed down through families," Nancy said, confusing Frances. "Skin disturbances like pimples are masquerades of sorts—elaborate and loud, wouldn't you say? Like the costume of a clown."

"I don't know a clown," Frances trailed off, and a silence ensued, with Nancy fussily picking spots of lint from her skirt.

After some time, Frances found words for her worries, and they poured forth. "I have a big scar, Nancy!" Blindly, she leaned over her leg, which she made bare in a single motion, sweeping her skirt away. "See how bumpy and awful it is? But it doesn't hurt. Palmer said never mind the scar; he says it's a common occurrence, that it's not serious; he's downright cheerful about the scar, so I don't mind it either . . . What do you think? Palmer doesn't think the scar will prevent me from maturing or leaving town. But, Nancy, I'm concerned that it might take over my will!"

The woman nodded scantly, remotely, as if behind a baffle of thought.

Then Frances fell upon what troubled her even more. "Oh, Nancy, tomorrow is the dance, and I just can't bear to go! I won't be able to make it."

"A dance!?" The woman seemed to awaken, yelling with a strange, light joy, laughter impelling the animated, switching movement of her large eyes. Nancy enjoyed festivities, Frances knew. Years before, she had spied a tiny piñata hanging above Nancy's oven, though the ornament had disappeared nearly as long ago.

"But I don't like dances, Nancy!"

"Oh no? Well, then — " The woman flipped a hand, exhaling, setting the cigar on the end-table, sinking deeper in her chair, " — don't go."

Life sounded so easy when Nancy spoke of it.

Frances suspected that Nancy lived a life different from any before ever known, a vastly comfortable, intelligent life that would be impossible for anyone in Munson or Little-Munson to understand, let alone replicate. And in Nancy's wide, lipsticked smile, there was no trace of competition, defensiveness, or malice, though there seemed something in her fiber that helplessly drank in and digested the turmoil of others.

"Frances, are you upset because you care for Doctor Mark Carol?"

"Nancy!! You know him?"

The woman's silence gave Frances the answer.

"Don't you see, Nancy!? When someone likes me, I simply reflect the affection back to them and even magnify it!"

Nancy raised an eyebrow.

"... So even if I don't like Doctor Mark Carol, it somehow turns out that I do! Oh, Nancy, do you want me to attract and marry him, the way the rest of the townsfolk do?"

Very slowly, with a movement beginning infinitesimally, Nancy shook her head slowly, lips parted, appearing puzzled, thinking hard, relaxing further into the chair, her rigid, shell-pink ears attuned with such credulity that Frances grew sad.

But as minutes crept by, she became irritated with Nancy's static-laden hair, calm remarks, and comfortable furniture. Still looking puzzled, Nancy stretched her stockinged legs to rest upon a soft hassock between her chair and the sofa. In a sudden spirit of play, Frances extended her own legs upon the hassock too, grinning as they struck Nancy's bony, lumpy shins. With a confused, myopic gaze, Nancy tried to withdraw her legs so slowly that the unpleasant dryness of stockings and skin scratched along Frances' legs, even as the woman completed the movement with a sudden jerk that made her hair fly. And with a stubborn impulse rising inside her, Frances pushed her legs hard on Nancy's, pinning them fast to the hassock while the woman tried again to yank her long legs away.

"What the hell are you doing?" Nancy rasped, breathing with effort.

Frances giggled, then suppressed a large grin to the floor. It was difficult to explain the joking with the legs. "I don't know!" she cried, swelling into giggles again.

Nancy grimaced, flashing angry eyes as Frances lifted her legs and flung them again on Nancy's, and Frances laughed hard through her nose, enjoying the sensation of teasing Nancy. Lips angry and compressed, Nancy pulled a leg free and used it to push the entire sofa, with Frances upon it, backward. The sofa lifted. Nancy stiffened her legs and arms with the effort, appearing like a large doll, Frances thought. Then the big piece of furniture crashed back to the floor. Nancy looked disgusted. "Will you please—"

Frances raised her hand to indicate that the joke would now stop, despite the fact that the women's legs were again joined in an uncomfortable tangle that grew heavier, and seemed to form the type of lock that, with the passage of time and weather, becomes difficult to break. The heel of Nancy's shoe fell off. She reached to retrieve it, and in doing so slipped from her chair and bounced onto the floor, her legs still elevated on the hassock, entangled with Frances' legs. Nancy gave forth an angry mewl and the two women began the struggle again, with the adhesive sound of the legs on the vinyl hassock filling the room. During the leg-struggle, the absence of normal discussion with its punctuative starts and pauses made time seem to change, Frances noticed, as did the finer characteristics of both women's personalities. Denatured and smooth, they each grew tranquil and new; Frances stared at the folds and planes of Nancy's face for a limitless moment. Then Nancy kicked Frances hard on the toe.

"Nancy, it was just a—a comic joke," Frances gasped to explain. Their legs fell from the hassock.

"What? WHAT?" Nancy stared crossly at a point somewhere between the couch and the floor. She stood and hobbled back to her chair.

"Calm down, Nancy? Can't you stop—" Frances' body tightened with embarrassment, eyes thick and teary.

"You tell ME to stop? What are you SAYING, Frances!? Sit there and do not move! Move not a bit!"

Frances slid down in the couch, shuttering her eyes.

Now Nancy tucked her legs beneath her, adjusting her skirt. "What in Christmas were you thinking?"

"I'm usually thinking of pleasant things," Frances

said defensively, though Nancy did not seem to care for this reply. An oily tear slid down Frances' cheek, and she guessed Nancy would soon expel her from the room, so to avoid such a scene, she gathered her smock around her and stood, preparing to leave.

"Now what are you doing?" the woman demanded sternly.

Frances sat again, weeping lightly, and then noted with relief that Nancy's eyes were empathic. The woman was not really angry. "Oh, Nancy!" she burst forth. "I'm never really sure what I'm doing or who I am! What on earth am I going to do tomorrow? Go to the stupid dance? I'd rather travel for days without food to find the chicken-beak oil—"

Nancy regarded her with a fond half-smile.

". . . Am I like you, Nancy? I wish I could be! I don't have a role in life: you do—you're an adult woman and mother. All folks—Kenny, Mother, Mal, everyone—want me to meet Doctor Carol at the dance. They want me to kiss him and more!"

"Well, that may be so, Frances—"

"Maybe they're right. Nancy, if I don't kiss him tomorrow, why, this whole town might break into pieces."

Nancy raised the eyebrow again.

"Oh, Nancy, I never liked riding around in cars at night or sneaking to the beaches to swim like the others. I hate shopping on Saturday mornings with mothers, I hate sandals and short sets, town meetings, socializing, and there's no way out of it! Don't you see that I just like to stay at home?

"But even then, I do wrong things, Nancy, like picking all the skin off my lips, for instance, or having coffee and pills enough to make me near-crazy! I know I should leave Munson for good, but I'm divided into two sides—and Nancy, do you know there's a local fireman who feels much the same way?

"I can't look for the oil and go to the dance both. I've never had to choose before, do you see?"

Nancy quietly slipped her feet into a kind of soft, shapeless slippers which, lined amply with clotty white fur, were stowed beneath her chair. Eyes slightly crossed, smiling with warmth, Nancy stood. She spoke so directly and off the subject that Frances was stunned.

"I must travel south today, not terribly far, to a crockery shop on the highway. There I will buy a Dutch oven. Why? Because, you see, dear Frances, tonight I must prepare dinner and next day's lunch for my entire family. They are driving to Munson tomorrow, the lot of them. This makes me nervous, because I want everything to be right! Frances, they are part of me."

"Oh!" She grasped the sofa edge, forgetting herself, fervid at the thought of Nancy's family eagerly chewing a supper cooked by Nancy alone. What sort of people could they be? The thought of Nancy preparing so industriously for the visit brought Frances to a kind of precipice, and she listened on, rapt. ". . . I'll finish cooking at midday; then clean my car of debris—the raisin, and other junk," the woman said, eyes slick, overlarge and jumpy behind her glasses' lenses. "Then I'll wash the fenders. I just can't think of disappointing my family with a dirty automobile or poor cooking . . . It means an enormous amount of work. Frances, can you help? Come tomorrow, early; can you? We'll breakfast and then get right to it. All I have done so far is put the pot roast into a soaking tub of vinegar and salt . . . gosh, what else will I need?"

"But Nancy! What about the dance? What about my decision?"

"You're not the only one with problems, Frances," Nancy said, distracted by a scrap of paper in her hand covered with excited-looking, crabbed handwriting and a sloppy chart of numbers.

"What's wrong with you, Nancy?"

"Wrong? Well," the woman breathed on, studying her list, "that's a good question."

Frances had never before heard the smarting hook of worry in Nancy's voice.

"Do my petty concerns surprise you, Frances?"

She nodded, almost in tears.

Frances slumped over the couch's arm, staring downward, deeply imagining Nancy's family, feeling both rejected and in need of sleep. Surely the family was a group of vital folk with large appetites who enjoyed all of life thoroughly; and perhaps right now the group was rolling along roads from a distant city toward Munson, loud-voiced and raucous, with countless hobbies and interests that Frances would never understand, and in the end, she found the family rather unbearable, simply because it existed at all.

"Are you an auto-owner, Frances?"

She raised her head. "Why, no; should I be? There's nowhere to drive—" Her gaze dropped again and scavenged the room's sandy-beige carpet with its redundancies of swirls and piled bumps like sandless dunes.

Nancy smiled flutteringly, eyes lightly teary. "Well, it doesn't matter. I can go on the other errands myself. I know I've never told you before . . . but sometimes,

Frances, I need help awfully in my life."

"I can see that!" Frances shrieked, inflated with anger. She rose uncomfortably, ready to leave, legs trembling to match the shakiness in Nancy's voice; then she glimpsed Nancy's right hand, delicately cupping great numbers of straight pins, and when the hand unfurled, the pins dropped, flashing through the air like a single skein and breaking into shards on the floor.

She fell back to the couch, muddled. "Should I really help you clean and prepare for guests? But what about the dance? Oh, you're weaker and more needy than I ever imagined, Nancy . . . messy, too," Frances mumbled softly into her chest in a rather high register, head swaying indefinitely. "I always thought Nancy so strong, firm, and independent . . . so different from me . . . that's why I liked her."

And now Nancy seemed to be moving softly, lighting candles, drinking a tumbler of water, sighing, straightening papers, checking for a dial tone on a palm-sized telephone; and Frances, turning her face into the sofa and back, presently gazed through the wide window at the buttery-pink edge of sun, which smeared light upward as the sky grew yellower and more ready, it seemed, to accept the enormity of the bright morning.

Frances wanted many things. She wanted to stay home from the dance, yet she wished to attend it too, so she could be part of things, and not disappoint the town. She wanted to travel and find the oil for Palmer; she also wanted the unnameable delight of observing Nancy with her relatives. She wanted to clean the car of debris, including the raisin, and to labor at every chore possible again and again, not just tomorrow, but on all days, for the simple reason that Nancy might wish it. With eyes now feeling coated and gummy, she settled into the sofa with short, soft movements, and in the colors of the morning, Frances reached for the woolly coverlet, pulling it to her chin with the sofa's rough texture behind her neck, then slept unknowingly.

*   *   *

She woke in grainy-gray dimness. Nancy, she said to herself at once, then realized the woman was gone. The pillow, linty and suffused with a lingering scent of cheese, was unappealing. Frances raised her head full of sleep, groaning, then realized with relief that she had slept long hours without the assistance of pills. Against the wall she saw a sack of dry leaves, then blinked: she was not at Nancy's house after all, but in her own bedroom. She rolled in the bed, looking to the window; the hour was either drastically early or stupendously late, she could not tell, but the present moment seemed off-kilter nearly to the point of being forbidden.

"Ray! Coffee! Please?" she called. Ray did not answer. She dropped back to sleep.

A door slammed.

"Hullo, Frances." Ray was busy with chores. "You stumbled in earlier. I heard someone outside—and a motor, and a lady's voice . . . You closed your curtains and went right to sleep when you came in!"

"Oh, I remember. Gee, this fog!" she cried, looking around, disoriented, tongue thick. Frances recalled with a jolt that tomorrow she would have to decide whether or not to go to the dance. A swarming, circling sensation pressed in.

Ray held a rake. "What?"

"Oh, Ray! I slept all morning!"

"You'll begin to feel better," he assured her. "It's easy to lose one's bearings. For me, too, sometimes."

"I know," she answered from the blanket, "Why is that, d'you suppose?"

His brow furrowed. "Don't know, Frances. It just is."

"I learned something strange earlier, Ray: Nancy has her own life. Oh, it made me feel so strange! I should have known she had a family . . . How stupid . . ."

Ray dropped his weight on the bed beside her. "Frances, I've been wondering about you lately. You've been on your bicycle, riding around a lot."

"What of it?"

"I want to know something. Frances, are you content?"

"You've never wanted to know such a thing before! Why now, Ray?" Tears welled, and Frances churned cold legs beneath the bedclothes, aware that she was overemotional right now, and had been for some days.

"It's something I've been mulling over."

She sat up. "Are you really worried about something so insignificant as my contentment?"

"It's part of a larger interest. Tell me, Frances."

But she could not. Frances pulled the curtain and gazed through the window at the lawn with its grasses shifting, rippling in the sun, perhaps from the below-ground comings and goings of beetles or infant mammals. "Ray, isn't it fascinating though true that life is so complicated we can't see other people clearly, for who they are, at any given time?"

"Well . . . I see you pretty clearly, Frances."

"Oh, really? Then you should know if I'm content or not."

He shrugged.

"Even if folks everywhere had good lives, Ray, I bet they'd invent all sorts of imaginary troubles to explain why they most frequently feel rotten."

He regarded her narrowly. "Frances, my idea is to count heads. See how many folks in Munson really are content, or not."

She snorted. "What a ridiculous idea, Ray! No one around here is going to answer that question. They're too afraid of how their answers will sound to the others. Oh, this town eats at me, I tell you." She twisted her fingers. "Sometimes I think I'll crack!"

"A tally of individual responses would form a picture, Frances, a map, if you like, for Enoch Ruth and the town council to see. Why, a single map can change the course of events—it's happened before."

"When?"

"Gosh, Frances. In the Civil War, for one thing."

"What a dope you are, Ray! What does that matter now? And if Munson folks say they're content, how can you believe them? They'll say anything to protect the town and its atmosphere." As she spoke, Frances felt a dismaying degree of despair that she tried to shake, banging her wrist on the bedside table. Could Ray be serious about the tally?

He said softly, "It's a legitimate question, and one I mean to look into. With a map, we can confront the town council with the problem. Is Enoch Ruth really content?

Is Mark Hodgkins? Mrs. Mars? We'll find out one by one, then ask the council to address it. Me—now, actually, I'm in the middle range."

Frances turned her face into the pillow. She longed for something—as on the night of the hayride—with an intensity so strong it seemed separate from her, and solid too, like a machine with workings of its own. The fog was swirling around the room, she noted, as if to dissolve the machine with cold and salts; words from her mouth softened the sheet. The yard outside, she knew, crawled with markers of life: rodents, gnats, silverfish, fallen whiskers; the trees' seeds blew in from the town's empty edges like sea-foam. She held the blanket and dug her body deeper into the bed, trying to affix herself there.

"I think of contentment as a string stretched horizontally above our heads," Ray was saying, "very high, such that we must try to reach it by jumping in the air. I usually can jump about two-thirds of the way up. If I could reach the string itself, or even stand atop it—! But I can't. There's always something in the way."

"Suppose someone saw fit to destroy the string," she asked, "by shooting it down?"

Ray frowned. "Gee, who would do that?"

"I don't know. A sheriff?"

He grinned. "Ha! A Munson sheriff. Well, if the string of contentment broke . . ."

"The usual kind of contentment wouldn't be important anymore," she said.

"I bet some folks are against the string of contentment, Frances, or they'd want to place it way up, too high. That burns me! Who doesn't want to try to live comfortably and content?"

"Ray," she broke out, "your map isn't going to do a darned thing. Oh, if I could just get a decent night's sleep and some soft, tasty food! I wouldn't mind some burnt coffee, either; the bitterest I can stand, the bitterest in the state! Haven't you made any today?"

He shook his head slowly, eyeing her.

"Why not leave Munson, Ray—come with me!?"

"I couldn't do that."

"Then should I stay here, with you?"

His eyes were red.

"What's the matter, Ray?"

"Are you going to marry Doctor Carol, Frances?"

"Oh, dammit!"

They waited.

"I don't think so—how do I know what will happen?" she said finally. "Would you care in the least if I married him, Ray? How do I know you wouldn't be relieved?"

"Don't you know the answer to that, Frances?" Ray answered sadly.

They lay back on the bed, and she rubbed against Ray tiredly with her head as she plunged toward sleep. Dozing, rolling, waking, Frances saw Ray scrunched at the far side of the bed, mouth agape in sleep, arm extended.

Ray stirred. Frances woke with an unpleasant taste in her mouth, the room enormous as a field without horizons, bearing upon her. Does the terrible size of this room merely indicate my own small, true size? she wondered. Frances looked up. Ray was watching.

"When I wake I'm not sure where I am," she muttered.

She roused herself. "The string of contentment . . ." she said. "You're fond of it, aren't you, Ray? You like the idea of struggling against something that challenges you—even if it's merely a string!"

Ray rubbed his eyes. "Yes. Sometimes instead of walking down Ann Street, I imagine I'm actually on a Roman road, carrying a sword, delivering an important message to a lieutenant."

"There's a sense of fighting most everywhere," she exhaled.

Ray stood with the rake, yawning, shuffling from the bed. "By the way, Frances, someone called for you earlier—a girl."

She looked at him for a long moment, uncomprehending.

"What's wrong?" he asked. "Did I say something off-key?"

"What girl?"

"I don't know—the caller said the word 'sickness,' then seemed to regret it."

"Oh, Ray, that was no girl—it was Palmer! You know his voice is naturally high and smooth! Don't you recognize your own doctor on the phone?"

"Hmmm. I saw Palmer yesterday, for an extraction. I don't believe the caller's voice was his, Frances."

Her eyes filled. "Could someone have been calling about Missie?"

"That dog isn't coming back. It's—"

"Was it Nancy?"

"Who's Nancy?"

She cast him a glance of disgust. The telephone rang then, its rich vibratory swell traveling through the living-room and mingling with Ray's voice as he asked another question, one she ignored. Racing into the hall, she fell upon the black instrument whose surface was covered with mars and hairlike scratches; the earpiece emitted a squeal, immediately followed by Palmer's voice. "—when it is not cold, but uncharacteristically warm, the air being protected, I think, by tree-leaves, though I could be wrong. But I've been wondering—"

"Palmer!" she cried. "—Did you call earlier? Ray said a woman called."

He did not seem to hear. "Frances, I'm thrilled at the prospect of our working in concert to make the balm. I can't stop thinking about it at night! Oh, I've a hunch this balm might well be a hit. It's going to have a lovely odor, you see." The smile faded from the physician's voice. "Your journey tomorrow could be cumbersome, Frances. Have no illusions! You mentioned some resistance in town—in your family—to your leaving."

She sighed. "Yes, Palmer."

"There's something you can do."

"Really?"

"Two things, actually. First, tell your family to change! Do this tonight."

"But Palmer! How? That's the very reason—"

"It may seem odd, Frances, but often, it's the most direct solutions that shine gloriously! I know this from my work in podiatry. See, when your family changes, other townspeople may take the cue, and the whole town's outlook may shift. This is how change occurs."

She breathed angrily, dubiously. "What's the second item, Palmer?"

"Think about pepper."

"Pepper!?"

"In small, frequent amounts, it lends vigor. Consider

it. Tomorrow I'll give you some more information about procuring the oil. Your journey is going to help us both, Frances." He hung up.

She replaced the receiver, and a half-ring erupted from the phone; she lurched forward, but the sound ceased.

Smoothing her smock, she drifted down the porch steps to her bicycle. There was no guarantee that Nancy would be available now, Frances knew, grabbing the handlebars, but she could think of little besides Nancy's starchy, scratchy sofa, which seemed to offer immunity from conflict, and she decided to ride to it.

Nancy was always so different from Frances. Her pleasant, precise mannerisms, along with the tendency to tell anecdotes more than once, were foreign to Frances. The differences between the two had deepened widely over time, Frances reflected. Now there existed a crevasse—a stark one, filled with something blinding as light—separating the two women, yet somehow Frances did not mind it. Nancy's plump fingers often sliced the air abruptly in a gesture unlike anyone's in Munson.

Ray came up the porch steps with another brimming bucket of water.

"Where are you going?" he asked.

"Can't you be quiet?" she cried, dropping the bike, running back inside, shoes pounding the floor, a slurry of grogginess rising in her.

"Oh—!" she cried, falling back against a doorjamb.

"What in the world are you doing, Frances?" Ray set the bucket down.

Fatigue sluiced through her: she was too tired to leave the house.

Frances lay in bed, eyes plagued by specks. Within a

short time, she had grown to know Palmer in a way she never imagined; she had also decided to leave her home. She was tired. Were Palmer's suggestions astute? If her mother's opinion changed, would her father's, too, insofar as her father's thoughts were embodied by her mother's, and, subsequently, might the whole town change? The idea caused her heart to knock.

When she woke, Ray's silhouette hung in the bedroom's door frame. "I slept all day," she said lifelessly.

He spoke through the darkened room. "That wild cabbage plant—I cut it away. It's dead now, Frances, so you don't have to worry."

"I wasn't worried!" she cried, irritated, flipping over in bed. Nothing hurt Frances. But she felt all wrong. Inching a hand to her upper leg, she fingered the scar's bumps and ridges, which were sore; asleep again, she dreamed of the green seed-pods mounded softly against an auto tire, and woke later to find Ray lightly snoring next to her.

Rising in the rumpled smock, she pressed her face against the bedroom window, then raised it, breathing in the yard's nighttime air. Living creatures by the dozens, it seemed, ran through the bushes. Lemurs, or what looked like them, sprang smoothly over the heads of thinner, lankier animals whose small eyes glowed like aluminum. The animals surged through the foliage to and from a gnarled apple tree at the rear of the yard, whose branches hung across the back alley. The alley was probably a gathering place for creatures who hunched in groups, maintaining stores of food or developing plans to survive at any cost. Frances' eyes widened as they met the steady gaze of a badger or beaver; then the animal quietly melted into the stream of others pressing through the yard. She heard a step.

"Missie?" she called softly, wondering.

"Frances!" A voice whispered from below.

A head moved below the window ledge. "Frances, a doctor named Mark Carol has moved to town."

"Kenny, what are you doing here?"

Kenny snacked on a cracker. "Everyone knows it," he continued, munching. "Carol is a classy professional— different from most men we know. He's got a terrific future, too."

"Yes," she said exhaustedly. "Everyone seems to be talking about him."

"He's handsome!" Kenny said, swallowing. "Did you see his curly hair?"

"No."

"Do you think you could care for him, Frances?"

"Why do you ask me this, Kenny?" she hissed.

"Because he's handsome and could change your life for the better! I'd feel so good if you and he were together. Besides, Ray ought to learn that he can't have everything he wants in life, including you! Come visit Carol with me now—what do you say? He's dining tonight at the Blue Top restaurant; I'd like to go." Kenny's eyes beckoned.

"The Blue Top!? Oh, I can't stand that place!" she cried. "It smells like old milk."

"You can't afford to ignore your destiny."

"I have a boyfriend, Kenny. Or haven't you noticed?"

"Oh, Frances. Ray is nothing like Doctor Mark Carol. Ray isn't successful—some say he's in his own world. And sometimes, Ray's mean!"

"Aren't you somewhat mean yourself, Kenny?"

She looked again to the mantle of hedges and plants at the rear of the yard and the apple tree, sensing the cool, muddy, living scent. "Oh," she cried, "what is happening?"

Years ago, before Kenny or any of her peers had been born, Frances wandered one night beyond the back alley to a neighborhood field that was now gone, its soils washed away. She recalled that in those days she knew almost no one besides her family, and walked often, dreaming elaborately of defeating bullies at school. That night, the dry grass of the expansive field was dotted with small fires, and Frances was content to watch them burn. The flames jumped closer, stirring insects who understood they must flee across the scrubby terrain. Then Frances saw, at a short distance across the fires, a plain, straight-haired girl in a plain dress whom she did not know and hated on sight, for the girl watched the insects in the same manner Frances did, quietly, with a vague air of superiority concealing tumult and distress. Like Frances, she wore short hair with a pleated skirt-set, and her silent presence nearly undid Frances, who tried to think of some way she could goad the girl into changing her appearance or even running away, so Frances would need never see her again. Finally she just shouted to the girl, telling her she would always be alone on the earth.

"Carol arrived in Munson two days ago," Kenny said, "in order to find a career and a mate."

"Kenny, that's simply disgusting!"

"Well, he has needs, Frances; and what's wrong with that?"

"I need things, too, Kenny."

"Exactly! Mark Carol is special. Now, it's true he's new to the region, but folks have already discussed this, and we realize he is a fine man through and through. When we meet him tonight, we'll order an ice-cream!"

"Why not call Curly-Dawn and your fireman friends and bring them along?" Frances said nastily. "They could all clamor after Doctor Carol, each trying to claim him as a best friend or fiancé!"

"What has gotten into you? Frances, you make it sound like our intentions aren't good. Don't you understand that this may well be the perfect moment to improve your life? Anyway, Curly can't come—she's ill from some mushrooms she picked. She's home in bed."

"Curly got poisoned?"

"Only a little, Frances."

She turned back to the bedroom, watching Ray roll over in his sleep, teeth clacking. She looked down to Kenny again. "Goodbye," she intoned, lowering the sash.

"Wait," she heard him call.

Ray's head sank deeper by degrees into the bed-pillow. Frances took a hard chair and gazed at her hands.

She saw the rake tilted at a hard angle against the bedroom wall. I hate no one, and I will gather my wits, she thought, while a ragged drowsiness crept in. If I sleep, will my life disappear?

She looked again at Ray. His skull was large, and Frances sensed, as before, that he was a stranger. Why couldn't he be a bit more like Doctor Mark Carol? Chin dropping, she slept. In a dream, she reached for a mug of coffee hot enough to blister her hands, and with a floridly polite gesture, she handed the mug to someone, but whom? The recipient wore a peacoat, and had, instead of a face, dry leaves.

If only night could become a permanent condition, obliterating the necessity of rising each morning, she found herself wishing from inside another dream, an overly active, exhausting one where long-limbed red birds cried above the sun while folks trudged down Ann Street below. She wished she could manipulate night, with its gradations of grays and bottomless darks, to stretch it into day as with a putty, to seize its capacity to induce sleep. Yet to hide in troublesome night wasn't possible, she knew. Half-waking, she fretted because she feared this day; already, streaming perfusions of yellow sunlight and the uncharted fog were swarming the bedroom.

"I don't like this feeling," she said toward Ray.

Awake, she rubbed her arms violently. "Why does the future matter so much?" she muttered. Frances did not like to know. Why was Mark Carol so powerful? Still in the hard chair, she conjured his handsome face willfully, as if in some rebellion against herself, and in her mind she dove toward him, sleepy again, hands open, stretching, excited. What was Mark Carol? A pressure jutted in her belly, and she lifted a blue drinking glass from the dresser, swallowing water avidly, imagining the scene of a wedding night between herself and Doctor Carol with all townsfolk standing above her, tearily happy. With his strong hands, teeth, and hips in mind, she half-stood, then sat back on the chair, dangling the glass that would shatter any moment to ice on the floor.

The sound of Ray's breath roused her. Frances opened her eyes and then set the glass gently on the floor; as an aid to try and sleep again, she tried to imagine tasty foods such as gravy and hard nuggets upon a cool lettuce-bed. On faraway continents, sleep connoted removal, paralysis, or death; that notion bothered Frances. The chair adhered to her cold legs like tacky syrup, and shifting again, she realized she would experience this day, the day of the dance, fully from within the fog. Deep bands of morning shadow now flared across the bedroom wall, along with tendril-like, silvery reflections shot there by the mirror, and these shapes formed to Frances a kind of brief, exclamatory story of a type she never had seen before, like a communication without words, or a photograph with no recognizable images; the shapes were exhortations and points of the story that changed as seconds passed along with the sun. Nothing could alter the story's course or rewrite it.

She heard a muted rumbling outside. Windows rattled.

"That shitty volcano!" she whispered hatefully, standing, fully awake, filled with fury.

"Goddammit!" Ray muttered from the bed, deep in sleep, enraged.

She waited, but nothing further happened; after some time, Ray turned thickly in the sheet, as if mired. "Don't get up," she said. But he was asleep.

Now the morning's full sun struck the room janglingly. The out-of-doors is terribly powerful, Frances thought, rising to switch on the same blithe, tinny radio music Palmer enjoyed in his office. Treading to the kitchen, she picked up a bottle and drank down some gray medicine she saved for special circumstances; lifting her chin, she drank faster, like a girl in a fairy story swallowing the potion that will transform. Moving to the living-room, she positioned herself directly over a few of the deep, mushroomy-smelling crevices of the sofa, dropped down, and slept.

*　*　*

Ray stood at the foot of the sofa, blinking out the sunlight. "I have chores to do for your lawn."

"What time is it, Ray? I need dark coffee."

"It's not early, and your coffee-taking is much too frequent, in my opinion, Frances. Do you really need more sleep?" he asked, apparently in a mood. "Kenny was here just a minute ago. You didn't wake."

"Oh?"

"He's gone now. He mentioned a meal tomorrow at Large Pete's Hotel—Doctor Carol is staying there for the time being, until he establishes a practice."

Frances pulled herself up between the poles of sleep and wakefulness, teetering, blurry. "Large Pete's? God, I hate that place! . . . Oh, Ray, don't you mind all this talk about Carol?"

"We can't stop it from happening, Frances. Carol is going to establish himself in town, and everyone is excited about it. I'm really not going to think about it."

"Ray!" she fretted. "Do you know what would really happen if I married Doctor Mark Carol?"

He nodded. "As a matter of fact, I do. He would put his hands right on your chest. That's how adults play around here."

"Oh!" she said tearfully.

"He might even do that in the daytime, while you're

both standing near the refrigerator."

"And don't you care that he would just step into town and marry me? Answer me, Ray!"

"What do you think? I care, Frances," he said slowly, eyes mournful.

"Then why did you introduce me to that man in the first place?"

"Someone . . ." She heard a catch in Ray's throat, a sound she had never before heard. "Someone would have introduced you two eventually. Frances, I wanted it to be me, not Enoch Ruth or Kenny or one of the others. Do you see?"

She pulled him to sit down. Ray smelled powerfully of celery, an odor that relaxed her. She pressed her nose to his shoulder.

"Don't wet my shirt, Frances."

"By God, can't we stop what's happening?" she asked, feeling herself beneath a burden.

"Even after you're married, you can borrow my dominoes," the man offered.

"Oh, Ray!" Tears came. Then warmth drained from her face and neck like silt, and Frances grew calmly grim.

"Maybe all those folks are right about Doctor Carol," Ray murmured. "Maybe he is best for you. I'm sorry, Frances. I'm no good. Kenny agrees."

"Of course Kenny does!"

"I don't like any of it," he muttered, touching his hip shyly.

"I wish the future would appear right now, so we don't have to wait for it like a bunch of dogs."

"Are you going to have a headache now, Frances?"

"Dammit, Ray! What if I do?"

"All lives change as we grow older and mature," he went on ruefully. "That's what folks say. I suppose ours must change, too."

Did Frances Johnson have an inkling about herself, her life-to-be?

"I should have left this town long ago," she said.

"The way people leave in stories, in the middle of the night? I doubt you could have done that." Ray smiled wanly, and lay back on the couch beside her.

"Ray. Did you ever simply want to fly away?"

"Sometimes. I like to think of new places to go," he said, toying with a gumball.

"Which places?"

"Well . . . to a different place, say, in a different era, where I could be like a hero."

". . . Sometimes, I've wanted to live inside a popular cartoon."

"Ha! So have I!"

"Or just to live in some other person's life, instead of my own . . ."

He turned on his side. "I've always wanted some big struggle in my life."

"I know."

"I mean . . . fight for the Kaiser or something."

"Don't talk about a battle, Ray."

"But it's true."

"Well, aside from a soldier, who else would you like to be, if only for just a little instant?" She grasped his wrist lightly. "A movie-star?"

"Well . . ."

"Just tell me, Ray—who? Please? Could it be Jerry

Welworth?"

"Ah, Welworth's all right, but he's not my favorite ac-
tor. No, I'm thinking of someone better. Hmm. Do y'
know how trumpet players march on the field?"

"Those who play in the marching band?"

"Yes," he said, growing quietly excited. "Band
members, well . . . they're on their own, yet they're part
of something, too. They just march along. It's not easy,
but it's not awfully hard!"

"Why, that's true," she said wonderingly.

"No one can disturb a band member or get them worried. They're protected by the whole group and their
instrument. I like it! They just play. They have something important to do. Band members are invisible, don't
you think, Frances? That makes them free. I've seen a
trumpeter—"

"Me too, actually! On the high school field."

"Yes! I watched him; he was just a faraway speck, but
I felt so close to him!" Ray breathed, his face mottling
with pink.

"I know that type of thing," she said. "It's a relief to
watch someone like that."

"Life didn't bother him at all. He had his job to do. He
just marched, part of the band, blending right in, and he
didn't feel worried or strained about anything. I wanted
to be him so badly!" Ray paused. "But later, Frances, it
was too much. I couldn't watch anymore. I wanted to run
away, never see him again!"

She waited. "It's good to think of other lives."

"But not any old life. Not someone from Little-
Munson."

"Why couldn't it be someone from Little-Munson,

Ray? I don't see why not."

"Well, they're troubled over there, Frances."

"Aren't you troubled?" She took his upper arm, squeezing it fondly, looking at Ray up-close, seeing him clearly, and Frances was glad.

He smiled. "No, for this game, it has to be someone good and right-minded. It could be someone living far away, like a man in the government. It could be a famous sportsman."

"It could be someone ordinary, but great."

"It could be a blind person," Ray said.

"It could be anyone, really."

*　*　*

Frances left the house, climbing on her bicycle. She had to visit Nancy, and felt far from rested. The bike pulled her across the grassy area behind Ann Street, which gave way to a large field of particularly gooey purplish mud, but Frances was not inclined today to turn back and take the longer, roundabout route. Stubbornly, she forced the bike through, watching the mud collect thickly along the wheels such that the extra weight drove the vehicle even deeper into the slimy substance. At last approaching Alt Road, she caught sight of thin, soft grass springing in trembling bunches from the pavement cracks, like the hair of infants, if such hair were green. She squatted to scrape the mud from the bicycle and her legs with a stick. At a signpost, she spotted a pay telephone.

A squalling sound emerged from the receiver, then, after she dialed, a voice.

"Mother?"

"Yes, dear." Frances could count on her mother to be home at virtually every hour.

"I want to tell you something."

"Oh no! Is it bad news? Not now, Frances, while I'm getting ready for the dance and your father is outdoors."

"It's not bad news," she replied.

"Wait, wait—I'll sit down." In the pause, Frances heard the sound of the wooden oars knocking together, creating a luscious, hollow sound.

"Mother," Frances said.

"You haven't forgotten about the dance?"

"No. It's about Munson. You said you don't ever want me to leave—and all the townsfolk seem to feel the same."

"Of course, dear. It would overstimulate you to leave home."

"But—Mother, I've already decided. I'm going to leave. Won't you change your mind and say it's all right? Then I can relax and stop worrying over what you think."

The mother's voice grew soft and cottony. "Why, when you put it like that! I suppose you're right! Have I been standing in your way, dear?"

"Well—" Frances stammered, nervous with the effort of the assertion.

"I'm sorry, darling!" the mother said. "It will be different now, I assure you. I'll stop bothering you. I'll change altogether—why, I'll change this afternoon. I'll tell your father, too. We didn't mean to upset you."

"Oh, Mother!" Tears of surprise and relief strained down Frances' face, and after wiping them she ducked her head into a bent arm, emitting a few blasting sobs.

Then she said into the receiver: "I'll leave on the journey soon, then. It's all part of an errand for Palmer, you see. I'm going to help him."

"Errand?"

"Yes—he designed an errand to help me! Well, it will also help him invent his balm. Oh, maybe it's not important anymore, but I'll go on the errand anyway—Palmer needs chicken-beak oil, and lots of it. I trust him now, Mother. Did you ever get to talk to him and trust him? It's not bad."

"An errand to help a man?" Her mother's voice turned shardlike, and suggested something sordid in the idea.

Frances squeezed the slippery-gray telephone receiver. "Of course it's an errand to help him. Can the oil be found in Florida? God, no! I'll have to travel across the state line for it, and it's going to do me a world of good. Once he invents it, the balm might help others, too, even folks beyond the state."

In panting breaths, the mother said, "What in heaven are you saying? Don't you see what this is? It's a ruse, that's what it is. That man is out to make a fool of you, and you're swallowing it like a soft lump of butter! What will people think when they see you traipsing up and down the roads—alone—for him?"

"I don't know!" she cried.

"It's an indecent errand!" the mother claimed. "A girl traveling alone, past state lines, on foot!? Is this on foot?"

"I suppose."

"An errand for a doctor on foot!?" The woman exclaimed, beginning to cry outright. "God! You know what everyone will think—"

"What? What will they think?" Frances cried, equally upset.

"They'll think that you're his mistress!" The telephone at the other end clattered to the floor, and Frances cried, too, beating the heel of her hand on her skirt, for the shame of it.

"You listen to me," Frances' mother said raspily, regaining the phone. "We're going to get you out of this. From now on, you're to focus your energies on Mark Carol."

"But what about Ray? What about the oil?"

"Don't mess around with me, Frances. You have work to do. Walk yourself right up to Mark Carol at the dance and start chatting. Oil? Oil doesn't achieve a thing, and neither does Ray Garn. But Doctor Carol will make something of himself. Of course, he's a newcomer, but remember, his aunt is Heidi, and everyone agrees that he is a fine man with a future and he's more than suitable for you. Upon occasion, you do listen to me, don't you, Frances? Then for God's sake, listen now!" The woman's voice vibrated with a timbre of ancient disappointment and bare nerves.

"Remember that Mark Carol is simply a good man with a marvelous station in life, someone who attracts good folk and succeeds at most everything he tries, and that overall, things are looking up for us today! He will add so much to Munson, too. Maybe, aside from his doctoring, he'll start a pharmacy business someday that will grow! Oh, there's no telling what he'll do, because he's really a blinding figure, dear. Try and attract his attention. Can't you?"

Wringing the phone receiver, rubbing its lower end

hard on her mouth in worry, Frances spotted, beyond the road's signpost, an ambling goose. "Well," she said dully. "I could try." It was true, Frances saw, that Mark Carol was a bit dazzling, and that the townsfolk, eager to know him, already had forgotten he was a newcomer.

". . . if you did. Have you flirted with him yet?" her mother was saying.

"No." She realized that the entire town was waiting for her to approach the new doctor.

"Well, don't worry," the mother said reassuringly. "Just like with birds, flirting comes soon enough."

Frances replied in a conspiratorial tone: "Mother, how much can we really know about this man? Couldn't he turn out to be immature, or a crook?"

"No, no, he certainly is neither of those things," her mother assured. "I think he is a busy, gifted man who has much to do and who might at times be businesslike, hurried, or gruff, but we understand this, and we help him as best we can. He'll be at the dance today, Frances; so will you."

"But Mother," Frances panted, "I have to tell you something. I've got a scar on my leg."

"That's fine, dear. Do you know who has a scar? Do you?"

"No."

"Your great-aunt had a scar; your grandmother had one, too. Your second cousin had one before her decease; and her sister has a scar on her elbow. And do you know who else has scars? Me! So don't worry. Your grandmother's scar was different than mine—rock-hard, it was, covered by a fleshy drape that looked like mucilage, and I believe it nearly ate her. What are ancestors for, dear?

Spots, dear, for passing little spots on to us, and that's about all. Oh, won't you cheer up?"

The mother seemed to move away from the phone and Frances heard the falling, clattering oars again, punctuated by a soft curse. "Medical science has names and classifications for these scars," she added, "whether they're gray, pink, mottled or what have you. But it really doesn't matter."

"Palmer didn't mention that."

"Well, Palmer wouldn't, would he? I never liked him. He's nuts! Thank heavens Doctor Carol is here."

"Mal Hide said the scar on my leg is a tumor!"

"Nonsense. What does Mal know?"

"Oh . . . Mother? . . . Why didn't you tell me about your scars before today?"

"Because they're not important, are they? Besides, dear, I couldn't have allowed a few little scars to speak for me, could I? I'm so much more than those scars. I need to show my children—everyone—my best side, after all. Now, do you feel better?"

Frances admitted she did. Clambering back upon the bicycle, she turned a wide circle and headed home.

*   *   *

She lay in bed, wishing a year had passed. Air breezed through the window, and, it seemed, the thin bedroom walls. There was so much to consider, Frances felt. Dangling an arm off the bed, she found a pan she had, in the past, used to mix house cement. Lifting it, she slowly spat.

Frances' mind could not stop. Inside her eyes she saw

her hometown and its low, white buildings and quiet streets, its climate both hot and cold with clouds of rainy, vertiginous swirls that made her recall, once more, high school and all the years long dispersed. When a teen, Frances had often been bubbly. Now she longed to relive those moments. Rustling in the bed, she thought her dissatisfaction with the present was not, contrary to what Nancy once suggested, a way to hide; and she thought Nancy would surely agree, if Frances could just explain it again one day soon. If she turned her eyes just so, she found the light in the yellow wavering sign of the unnamed hair salon at the end of Ann Street, open about three times per month. Perhaps the craving for high school days was nothing more than a wish to be safe.

"I am not quick on my feet," she spoke aloud dryly, thinking of a failed conversation so long ago after class with the attractive high school math teacher Mr. Luna, who had charmed Frances terribly once with a joke about a duck, and around whom afterward she still felt awkward. The man had been engaged to the high school's English teacher for several years, until both had died.

She noticed the weak odor of Ray's bagged vines somewhere nearby. Flopping over, she imagined there lived a vitality, some kind of force outside the window in the Munson air, a force that would yank at her tongue and change her, enable her to be truly impervious, stronger than Munson. Frances spat again into the pan. But how could such a force come from Munson itself? She sighed. "I believe every side, every point in an argument is of equal value, none more or less important than the next," she said aloud, suddenly sleepy, inhaling the damp taste of fog.

She kicked the thin, batterlike sheet enveloping her foot, not understanding how to know her life clearly, not least because most moments of life could not even be recalled. Since memories were not accurate registers of what was once real, was the wish to relive old memories, old moments, useless? The idea brought her back to Nancy's point. Was she trying to hide?

One afternoon when she was a child, Frances read a note scribbled in the torn family telephone diary that followed a long series of other telephone notes: "f. in bad humor, distasteful." Another day's entry read, "f. stole milk tart. now preening." Try as she might at the time, Frances had not been able to recall stealing a pastry, and wondered if the note pertained to someone else. Later, she still stood in the dim landing cradling the telephone diary, wondering if her father had written the entry, or her mother, or perhaps a visitor. She watched a windowsill where ants ferried items toward their home in the crumbling dirt outside, with their bodies' comportment of speed and neutrality. Frances heard her mother speaking into the upstairs telephone. "I've known her for years, and she is not a well woman. She lost a little boy, you know." The statement struck Frances, who jumped from the staircase and looked out the window for a disheveled, lost boy on Munson's streets, and did so many times afterward, but never spotting one.

Most of the time, her childhood home on Sarah Lane had been pleasantly quiet, with all the home's objects—each table, glass, and lamp—exceedingly still and motionless, perhaps due to some force of which the family had been unaware. The meager-pale, meaningless brown pattern on her childhood bedroom's wallpaper, always peeling, obscured images of human foreheads and eyes.

Frances had still been fairly young when, on a warm day, she lolled on her mother's white daybed, taking pleasure from the sight of her own legs. She squeezed the telephone receiver contentedly, dropping into a doze while waiting long minutes for an operator, because she had called a hospital in a faraway city to ask a rather pressing question. She woke from the doze, breath roaring against the damp receiver, to hear a hospital phone attendant on the line with the news that she would have to wait another ten minutes to speak to a telephone nurse, and Frances agreed, content to hang onto the phone, yawning, daydreaming, and refining her question with relish. She finally heard a buzz, then an opening of the line and the sound of footsteps approaching, then a warm, sympathetic woman's voice informed her, "Honey, you're out of luck!"—because all nurses had just gone home due to a newly approved citywide holiday, finalized only a few minutes before. Then the woman patched the line back to the phone attendant, to whom Frances blurted her question impetuously.

The attendant herself, as it turned out, happened to be a retired nurse of the Coast Guard, which she revealed after hearing Frances' question and snorting.

"Do you know where I can buy the wetted towelettes that so many folks are fond of?" Frances had asked, was driven to ask, she explained, because the product was no longer sold in the Munson pharmacy and could not be found on the grocery's shelves either. Once located, might she buy the packets in larger quantities, say, a dozen crates at a time? The attendant-nurse grew inexplicably irritated with the questions, and the whacking sound of a flyswatter or a strap traveled through the phone line. The only company that manufactured the towelettes Frances spoke of, very far away in another state altogether, had dissolved after a business crisis shook the firm to death, the attendant-nurse answered hoarsely, adding that it was strange that Frances had wound up on the line with this question, because the attendant-nurse happened to know about the company's failure only through a coincidence having to do with her family's roofer. Then the attendant began to needle Frances, chastising her for having a fancy, uppity attitude, and, like the final drilled notes of an assaultive song, the attendant-nurse gruffly told Frances to go find a washcloth, and use it judiciously with warm water.

*　　*　　*

She rose from bed with a surprising lack of fatigue, though she craved the sort of hot, acrid-bitter coffee that, if drunk too quickly, would scorch the tongue cruelly. Instead of cooking it, though, Frances hurried in her robe and white house-slippers down the porch stairs, taking advantage of her rested state to board her bike, which rolled softly over the grass as Frances went in anxious search of a clear space in which to breathe. The bicycle led her. Soon Sarah Park appeared, a green square naturally close to Sarah Lane. Abrupt, cold winds from the nearby volcano streamed across the still town, their moisture tugging at the strands of her hair; old leaves spun unreasonably into corners before gusting away in blasts of air.

Frances enjoyed the breezes. At a distance she glimpsed the tree-bare main street, its store windows reflecting the afternoon light. A legion of musky bats flew overhead:

she giggled suddenly, hand to her mouth. The bats' leathery flapping was so gruesome, spread above Munson's downtown! The hundreds of creatures all seemed in rough agreement with one another, flying jaggedly to an already-known destination, each free from the burden of decision making. They would likely land at a roosting center, where they would sleep undisturbed by discussion.

The bicycle gathered rich, clinging, dark green mud along its tires, an apparently new mud she had not encountered before. Frances climbed off to push the heavy apparatus through Sandy's Cut, a brushy area that provided a shorter route to the beach wall, then she hopped back on the seat, wheeling past the elevated cement ring and dilapidated park, racing down the hill through the old lumber yard that ran with scuffling mice, and in its speed, the bicycle flung the green mud from its spokes and tires. Spatters collected on her forearms' hair along with tiny wood shavings from the yard.

A few minutes later she was standing in Nancy's living-room, wiping her face with her hand, expressing severe dissatisfaction with life, crossing her arms, glaring, foisting her anger upon the silent woman. From a shoebox-sized radio on the floor at Nancy's foot, a music arose, broken piano chords anchored by a flute's melody that plunged forward too quickly, losing itself in a minute. Leaning onto a table beside the yellow sofa, Frances breathily began a list of complaints, beginning with the fact that Nancy's house was so far away from her own; her face grew steamy-pink, and she wiggled her toes in the wet, muddy slippers. Nancy gazed at her with blazing interest, green eye-shadow smeared like clouds across her eyelids, and she asked about Frances' sleeping problems.

"Do the pills help?"

"Oh, Nancy, don't talk about it! At one time in my life, I could fall asleep no matter where I was or what I was doing! But that was long ago. Yes, the pills force me to sleep well, when I take them. But my sleep isn't regular!"

"Must sleep be regular, Frances? With rules for governance and so forth?"

"Oh, stop it!"

"What about Munson's circle of rules, Frances? Do you feel safe inside it? Or . . . does it kinda bug you?" Nancy smiled goofily, legs outstretched.

She teared. "Nancy, Munson's rules are *my* rules too, because I'm from Munson. Besides, if I should ever disagree with the rules, other people would just die!"

The woman paused quizzically, eyes roaming, hands enwrapping the chair's armrests, face deep in thought.

"Do you think when I leave Munson, the rules inside me will fade? I doubt it! Oh, I've just got to go find the darned oil, Nancy! Won't it help? Gosh, the pressure! And in all this, do you really think I have time to help you clean your car?"

"I suppose you don't." The woman looked about to cry.

"Palmer was nice enough to offer the errand . . . and aside from carrying this out, what else can matter?"

Nancy's voice grew deep, smooth, and foreign as a mask. "Frances, never in a million years did I wish to trouble you with my own ideas and plans. Never mind helping me at home . . . tell me," she said, "what will you do when you leave Florida?"

Frances slumped into the couch, suddenly lethargic.

"Do departures make most people logy?" Nancy did not answer.

Frances took her chin in her fingers, squeezing. The room of softly colored chairs looked as quietly lovely as a jewel-box, with shifting spears of violet-orange sunlight from the window sliding across the wall. Frances' head dropped back to the cushion, tears seeping, because, in fact, she never wanted to leave Nancy's house again.

Would Frances Johnson ever savor the unknown?

Nancy remarked playfully, like a riddle or joke: "Suppose after you leave Munson, you are standing on the main street of another town with your suitcase. You see a young couple on the street corner, a girl about to kiss a boy's hand. What would you do?"

"Oh, God, Nancy, how do I know?" she answered lifelessly.

"Would you want to kiss the boy's hand too?"

"What?"

"If you could," Nancy smiled impishly, "would you?"

"Why would I?" She was annoyed.

"If you wanted a little kiss, or if you felt sexy?"

"Oh, Nancy! I'd probably kick them both."

"Oh?"

"Or I could press them awfully hard together so they couldn't stop kissing even to breathe, just to punish them for their kiss."

"Wouldn't you want to do any kissing, too?"

She rolled her eyes. "Oh, maybe. I suppose I would rather kiss his hand at exactly the same moment she kissed it."

Nancy's smile continued. "You mean you place your

kiss immediately next to her kiss, so that you would nearly be kissing both of them at once?"

"I might do that, yes, Nancy."

"Or you could suspend your lips directly above the boy's hand, but not quite kiss him until—"

"I could get the girl to stand behind the boy with me, and she and I could lock arms to kiss and exclude him. We'd step on his feet so he couldn't leave. I could tell them to go to separate street corners until I said time's up."

Frances' heavy mood lifted. "Nancy, it's true: I may enjoy a journey to a new town or city," she giggled, tapping the skin above her lip. Nancy broke out in a protracted, slurry grin.

The afternoon light was warm, and Frances breathed deeply, as if to stain her lungs with the air. "Nancy, isn't it funny to think that each person has a separate, beating heart? Wouldn't it make more sense if several people shared a central heart of some kind?"

"You mean to conserve biological energy and avoid life's loneliness both?"

Often, with Nancy, there was no need to explain. Frances lodged herself into the sofa, thoughts drifting; if only she could stay here with Nancy for weeks, their circuitous discussions orbiting around them always! They could go together, then, at their leisure, and wash Nancy's car of all debris, not once, but a thousand times, laughing, snacking on cold milk and crackers, dashing around the yard amidst piles of leaves and other dried plants.

Now Frances fixed her mind on the soft clock of her own breathing, sleepy thoughts wide as a sky horizon, the faint resonance in her ears of a bell. The next night's requirement for sleep, and the next's, suddenly seemed not a burden, but a detail. A mild fragrance unfurled through the room, caught in the swirling blades of a ceiling fan, a fragrance suggesting serenity and also butter, along with an intention so gentle and focused it broke into the air like humid flowers. The fragrance was in Nancy's dress.

She woke, gazing at the calm Nancy, who faced the radiator. "Oh, Nancy," Frances whined in grogginess, "can it be really true that every person in the world has a will of their own? That seems impossible."

"It does?"

"Some people are stronger than others. Sometimes ideas prove stronger than people, and stupid ideas are the strongest. Why? Atoms have a collective will. I wonder if dust has a will, too?" Frances scrutinized the furrows ringing Nancy's mouth, which deepened when the woman grew interested in something.

"Are you thinking of the dust among the figurines in your book-hutch at home, Frances?"

"Why Nancy! When have you ever seen my book-hutch?"

Nancy smiled. "You have a will of your own, Frances, believe me, though it may not appear or even feel real."

Frances cried, "I do?"

Nancy's voice was crisp and direct. "Frances, in choosing Mark Carol as a mate, would you actually, in a way, be choosing your mother?"

"What!!??"

She lurched from the sofa and plunged down the vine-infused front stairs, racing away from Nancy's house and down the slope toward a tiny, tricklish river that dwelt below a bigger river and Nancy's pebbled road. Without the bicycle, she ran too quickly, falling, scraping her knees; she stood again, embarrassed, defiant, uncertain of the time, wondering how much she must bathe before the dance, and, sensing that townsfolk everywhere were watching, planning, she realized suddenly that, in order to avoid peril, she must avoid her very self. Kneeling, Frances daubed silvery water from the smaller river upon her face, closing her eyes, and it occurred to her that the hour was growing late, though it could not yet possibly be suppertime.

*   *   *

Loosening her brown shoes, she progressed down the path, shifting her body into several versions of straight and slumping postures. Sun rays pierced through her vision and the misty-hot air made the Florida hilltops steam. Frances was worried. The dance had not yet begun, but she was late, and strove toward it inexorably, far behind Ray, Kenny, and the others who walked deliberately, dressed in formal, dark clothes. She saw a figure at a distance and peered: to her surprise, it was Mal's young friend Lucas, walking with an ill-at-ease woman, perhaps his aunt or mother. Usually, Little-Munson folks did not attend the Munson dance, because they hadn't the energy.

Frances frowned with irritation at her shoe straps, now wet, and her dark socks sagging at the ankles. She longed to be in her own living-room, lying down, the telephone at her side. Threading toward the back of Sandy's Cut, she moved down the wild embankment to a deeply wooded area with masses of straw along the road, impacted in gelatinous mud.

In the woods' hot mist she saw Ray and Kenny. "Are you two limping?" she asked, catching up. The brothers' habit of lurching was perhaps an inherited trait, or it came from the tendency of each to lean and bump toward the other as they argued and walked.

"Frances!" Kenny cried. "Will Morst said you might leave the dance early. And Mal said you might not go at all."

"What do they know about my plans?"

"Why, everyone knows you're talking about some drill out of town, Frances. I thought you'd drop the idea. It's so weird!"

She pinkened. "Kenny, don't you see that sudden, drastic plans usually take place for a good reason?"

"Well, you're here now, and ready for the dance, Frances. That's what counts."

"It's true I am planning a journey. It's not exactly a secret, but I doubt I'll talk to you about it!"

Kenny glanced at Ray, then at Frances' shoes. "Why would you do this, Frances?"

"I'm going to get the chicken-beak oil because Palmer needs it. Do you think I'd rather stay at the ratty dance the rest of the day and night? I even had the chance to help Nancy get ready for guests, but leaving on my own is the most important, don't you see?" As her heart thumped in anger, Frances was aware that she was once more pleading with Kenny, whose eyes smarted her with their alarm. "I'm putting in an appearance at the dance: isn't that enough? And if I leave early, well, it's no one's business."

"It's my business," Kenny answered, "because I worry

about you, Frances. Right now, your concerns are ours—Mark Hodgkins said so, and Tod Maria at the station, too. How can you leave town during the dance? It looks plain bad, Frances, and it hurts us all."

She turned in the hot sunlight to Ray, who was pulling his shoe-toe through some leaves. "Ray, I must talk to you in private, please." She took him by the arm.

"Wait!" Kenny yelled suddenly, sweat-dots on his face. "I am not a dispensable object to throw away whenever you two feel like telling secrets together—"

Ray raised his eyebrows. "Go across the path, Kenny. Or would you rather I tell all the firemen about your dream?"

Kenny glowered and went across the path to a fat tree.

Frances looked after him. "Which dream is that, Ray?"

"Kenny has dreams about wrapping up the other men in the firehose and kind of squeezing them, that's all."

"Oh, Ray, you wouldn't gossip that way to the firemen. Why are you mean to your brother?"

"I don't know." Eyes severe, he turned into the sun.

Then the cool fog unfurled inside her, and when she spoke it seemed across bright and dark chasms. "I'll be at the dance so briefly, I probably won't even see Mark Carol."

"Do you like him, Frances?"

"Dammit! Stop asking me that!"

"I'm just asking what other folks have asked . . . because they all want to see you happy, successful, and privy to life's best secrets," Ray said miserably.

She stared. "Do you know just who you are, Ray? Do

you like that person in the least?"

"Frances, be calm."

"I feel too large sometimes, lopsided and filled up with other faces and voices . . . I can't stand it!"

She knew Ray did not favor this kind of talk. But Frances could not help herself. "Have you ever felt that you were under siege, Ray?" she asked.

He shook his head. "The word 'siege' refers to really serious events on the world scale, Frances. Weaponry and hostages, frank violence, that sort of thing. Napoleon's venture inside Russia comes to mind. The capture of Moscow . . . Hmm, no, Frances, a single individual can't be under siege."

"Of course they can!"

He stooped to the ground, pinching a lump of mud. "It was one of Napoleon's worst moments, you know. A victory would have changed the world map. The Moscow winter—"

"I know! It killed his army!"

"Years later, he died—alone, in a rocky, remote place—"

"Ray!" she snapped. "We're not talking about Napoleon."

"—But on the last day of his life, in a little house, he was crazy maybe and he cried. He wrote a poem to his men who starved in Russia."

"Is that true?" Frances was suddenly touched by this description of the conqueror.

At a distance, Kenny made a hooting, gassy noise.

"A lone Florida girl can't be under siege."

"Ray, listen to me!"

"Maybe the siege is in your mind, inside yourself,

Frances. Ha! Maybe you made the so-called siege!" He grinned, glancing down at his fingers, long and yellowish as beans.

The idea was new to her, and Frances was stunned. Slowly, she lowered herself to the path and its hard, damp mud, sitting, legs loosely extended. "Could it be?"

" 'Course it could."

"A siege of my own making?" She inhaled as if to taste the idea. "How awfully strange! That a person can invite a siege without realizing it—thereby helping create it—is that what you mean?"

"Sure it is."

She was guarded. "How, exactly?"

"Frances, can't this wait?"

"Ray!"

"Well . . . folks could invite a siege by allowing it to happen, I suppose . . . or by asking for it a little! By being mixed-up. You're mixed-up, Frances."

"I'm not!"

He twisted a handkerchief.

"Ray, what you say gives me power!"

"Of course, real captives under a real siege fight their captors. This was true between the Russians and the Old Guard—"

"No, Ray, it's not true in every case, I'm sure it isn't. Captors and captives could become close. Where a siege comes from, there's always—"

From across the road, Kenny shouted exultantly. "Hey!"

Ray took her by the arm, pulling her up, a complicated expression on his face. "And where the hell does a siege come from, Frances? Where?"

"Here, here . . ." she whispered, limp as she rose up, looking to the sky, tears rolling back.

As the afternoon light and heat blazed, she heard Kenny at a distance, humming a salty marching tune.

*　*　*

A large gathering of flies clung to a bush, but did not buzz. From where she rested alone near a tree-stump, Frances heard a rustling above on the slope. Looking up, she glimpsed, through the trees and brush, an ordinary glass tumbler filled with brown tea. A hand held the tumbler.

"Palmer!" she called. "I told the others I'd catch up!"

He slid down the bushy embankment awkwardly, long shoes pushing beards of crumbling, flowing dirt; the man's glasses glinted through the trees as he approached. he cloying fog was with her fully. She felt as if she and Palmer were not quite present, that their flat bodies faced one another in the enormous container of the forest as if upon an artificial, echoing stage-set that happened to have, far above its muddy floor, a ceiling of green trees.

How would Frances Johnson negotiate this day?

"A reminder, Frances," the man said, breathing shallowly. "I'm looking forward enormously to the arrival of the oil, and to moving on with my work!"

"You believe in the balm, don't you, Palmer?"

"Yes!" The man seemed jittery.

"—Well, Palmer. I should tell you. I have a new power!"

"Power?"

"It's a type of insight. Ray showed it to me a few minutes ago, and it has nothing to do with being passive, or giving — "

"What are you saying, Frances?"

"I've been thinking, Palmer. I'm going to stand apart from Munson in my own way, and I don't need to journey for the chicken-beak oil to do it. Oh, I know you want the oil, Palmer. But today — "

"Ah, Frances," he said. "Don't you see? It's commonplace for people to believe they've alighted upon some tremendous power when in fact it's all a ruse!"

She tried to ignore the doctor, tidying her skirt.

"The oil will bring us luck, Frances — I believe the stuff is indescribable. Stick with me, please? In making the trip, you'll be able to put Florida behind you — and isn't that what you want?"

She was torn, swarmed.

"All you have to do is cross the state line and shop. You'll see many small feed-and-novelty marts on the side of the road. Or are they just before the state line? I can't remember. Once you see these stores, though, you can begin asking where the oil is sold. One of the stores is famous! The place doesn't really have a name, but a wooden sign at the entrance says 'I Too Must Die.' That's funny! They sell gifts, and pancakes, too. Behind that mart is a beautiful little algae pond — "

"Palmer, I can't go! I'm going to stay here and face the dance. I'll find out what I've been doing wrong. Of course, I've got to leave early and tell Nancy all about it, too."

The man looked disappointed to tears. "Ah, Frances, I thought I could count on you. I wanted you to make the journey most of all," he said, "because it would have meant we joined forces."

They waited.

"Say," Palmer said finally. "Do you know what a calliope is?"

"Calliope?"

"Few realize it, but that instrument's notes work peculiarly well at masking numerous other sound waves, including those of the human voice," he explained, gazing toward a group of lean trees. "Frances, I think with that calliope playing on the pavilion stage today, no one will hear you leave early for Nancy's house! In other words, the sounds of the dance itself will provide you a protective shield."

The fact that the dance was so close made her nervous. "Hmm. That's good, Palmer."

Where would Frances Johnson wind up?

She bent over low, a cramp in her ribs. "Oh, there's so much air to breathe in the forest. Must I take it all in?" She wheezed, grabbing at the man's pants leg. "I hate breathing . . . sometimes it's simply so ugly!" She opened her eyes to spy a large, honey-brown critter fleeing through the foliage.

"I agree that breathing is a little disturbing, if you think about it for very long. Perhaps it would help if you knew the reason all the animals must breathe? I can easily tell you."

"But Palmer," she wheezed, "I thought you didn't care about the meanings in life, whether for warts or the universe or what-not. You said the reasons are a waste of time."

Holding his chin in his hand, wagging his head as if ashamed, the doctor looked down to her. "Ah, it's true that we spend our lives wondering about the earth and sky," he said distractedly.

She wiped her face, breathing easier, turning to the hill. On the far side stood the pavilion, with the townsfolk's dressing shacks and sleepover cabins interspersed through the trees. "Palmer," she asked, "are moose bright?"

"Oh, they're fantastically bright," he answered immediately.

Now she took his arm companionably. "Do y' suppose that the food in the forest protects them, and all the animals who eat it?"

"I'm sure their diet is healthful for them, Frances."

"No, Palmer—I mean, does the forest have substances or properties—? Ah, I don't know what I mean."

They stepped through a hidden, small creek so cold it made her foot-bones ache. Frances sprang from the water, though the man did not seem to care and walked slowly.

She said, now facing him, "I think so much about myself that it's shameful. At the same time, I can't honor my own wishes!"

"How's that, Frances?"

"When I let others' wishes be stronger than mine, then—oh, Palmer, I just hate—"

"What, Frances?"

"I hate being a woman!"

"For the love of Mike! Why?"

"It just feels funny. Folks don't see me when I'm standing nearby, and they strike me accidentally with their arms when putting on their coats, for example, in winter." She bit the web between her thumb and finger. "I want to fit into life, Palmer: don't you?"

"Sure!"

"Well, do you know where you fit and who you are?

—Oh, you must. See, there are sides to life I've never experienced, like swimming in the ocean, or celebrating my birthday loudly. And if I let this town control me somehow, then I've got to stop it!"

"You're just confused, Frances. It's part of being young."

"Oh, dammit!"

She was sweating into her blouse. Frances struck out in the direction of the dance pavilion, angry, still worried about her lateness; she turned back to Palmer, seeking to ask just one more question—regarding how much of the universe is explicitly unknown—but she could not articulate it, and instead looked without speaking as the man turned and tripped over a stick, his mouth an open circle below the glasses tumbling from his eyes.

*   *   *

"Do you see that girl over there? Not too long ago, something terrible happened to her." Her mother combed Frances' hair with stiff fingers, standing behind her, pointing through the open cabin door to a petite woman in the clearing wearing a white, fluffy dress.

"What do you mean, something terrible?" Frances' mind lagged. She shifted on the vanity stool, a knot inside her like vague fear. The lengthy evening ahead was unknowable. She tried to find the new power, but thin and uncatchable, it slipped away somewhere in her mind.

From Mal's cabin on the forest slope she heard the vast, breathy notes of the organ warming up in the dance pavilion. Ray and Kenny stood near the cabin's open door, arguing tensely, Frances overheard, about the life-length of snowballs.

"You haven't heard about that woman who's standing over there?" the mother asked.

"How the hell would I? I don't gossip on the phone every minute of the day, do I?" Frances smoked now, inhaling fiercely once, sniffing as ashes flew up her nose, coughing explosively while the mother frowned.

She noted in the cabin's old yellowing mirror that she looked more attractive than usual. Frances' face was tinged with pink. Her eyes were highlighted. Though the thick, granular fog hovered close upon her shoulders like a stole, making her afraid, she tried to ignore it and remain outwardly calm. Yet, all folks would be watching her today. Wiggling slightly, she even sought comfort in the fog, pretending briefly that it was as unremarkable and soft as her own skin; she stroked her arms. At the cabin's dank vanity table, Frances hummed a shapeless tune, eyes darting and catching the fractured sunlight that glazed the clearing outside.

The mother continued, "You should recognize her—she's Linda Del-Adam, Florida's most celebrated dancer. How can you not know that?"

Frances grimaced into the mirror. Perhaps in the future, she would have no recollection of this day, much in the way she had almost no memory of town dances from her youth.

Would Frances Johnson ever be done?

". . . after that, and so naturally," the mother was explaining, "Del-Adam tried to kill herself and failed. She would have bled to death if a certain admirer hadn't come to her house that very night to take her to supper at the Cove restaurant."

"Why should that woman have wanted to kill herself?" Frances heard her voice saying, smeared inside the fog.

"Why, Frances? Why? Only because the man she loved was dead, and without him she couldn't see any reason for living."

"Can't you make sense?" Frances muttered as the mother pulled at her hair, then daubed it with a mudlike gel. "I have things on my mind."

"It makes perfect sense, Frances!" the mother said derisively. "Only you in the world cannot see the point of this story."

"I have important things to do today, and I'm afraid I might never do them!" She drummed her fingers on the tabletop scattered with cobwebs and ladies' abandoned trinkets.

"Oh, go on, Frances, with all your notions so dull to the rest of the earth! I'm telling a story full of life and color," the mother fumed, stretching the hair, combing its ends, "but you can't appreciate it! Those two were once a famous dancing team! Del-Adam simply couldn't go on without her husband. Luckily, Stuart Belinda found her before it was too late. Now, of course, Del-Adam has a wonderful life, and offspring."

Frances felt worn. "Who's Stuart Belinda?"

"For the love of misery! Don't you recognize the name Stuart Belinda? He's an extremely famous clown. Of course, he'd been in love with Del-Adam for years."

The sun, heat, and steam of the day combined with Frances' fog to create an oppressive admixture, inside which she strove to breathe shallowly. The dancer of whom her mother spoke now stole across the mud clearing in transparent slippers, veering shyly from Ray and Kenny, and on quick legs, she flew straight toward the cabin door, as if having sensed Frances' mother's interest. She poked her head closer toward Frances' head than seemed permissible.

The woman was doll-like, with a miniaturish, thin face, and the sparkly, diaphanous white dress puffed around her. She appeared even smaller than she was, since her voice was breathy and her hair wispy, and she addressed Frances and the mother. "Oh, I would love a little drink of milk! Where can I find one?"

"Good night, dear, I don't know!" cried Mrs. Johnson.

"You can't drink milk here. Why don't you go home?" Frances gibed meanly. She squeezed her eyes shut, lowering her head, for suddenly, all before her eyes—the besequined dancer, her mother in the mirror, the moldering boards of Mal's cabin—all were swallowed abruptly in a rush of the insolent, braggart fog, as if never to return. The fog changed the world more than she could have believed. It mocked her and tipped the floor so she would fall.

But her mother was speaking to the dancer: ". . . with a whole glass of fluid, dear, because milk is very good for the hair. In fact, all forms of milk are helpful to your hair, including whey. Have you tried whey? Few folks know this, but, oh, it's the stuff of dreams! I sit quietly and eat whey at special times—when I'm blue, for example, and after meetings. Oh, I've often dreamed that Frances might enjoy whey, just as do I, and I've hoped that someday she'd sit just so with her whey, like a beautiful picture of a young girl. But she never has!" The mother sighed, downcast. Suddenly, she brightened. "Why, Miss Del-Adam, just look at your arms! They are absolutely perfect, without a mole or freckle on them. The arms of a princess! Tell me, who finishes your arms? It must be a specially skilled medical man—could it be Doctor Carol? Oh, of course it isn't; he's just arrived in town. Rather, Miss Del-Adam, do you sneak away regularly to a big city to have your lovely arms done up?" The mother smiled with cloudless admiration.

Moving lightly away, facing them, the dancer smiled, bowed scantly, then leapt backward into the clearing, sunlight eking across her small frame. Her feet flitted like wings, and she stopped. "It's been a wonderful day thus far, ladies," she called airily. "As a performer, I need to look my best at all times, so now I must leave you: there's so much to do! I am not nervous about my little solo onstage tonight. It will be very brief, after all, just a way of saying 'hello' to everyone here in the language of a dance . . . and do you know, I love to think about the dances of past eras, the dances my parents attended before I was born? Sometimes I long for an evening scattered with stars to transport me back to a night when my parents were young! If I could do that, then, oh, I would be exactly where I've been longing to be all these years! We have every right to go back in time, don't we? Oh, I simply demand it!" She smiled, dropping her shoulders and arms so they sagged loosely for a moment. "Isn't it terribly ironic and hurtful that we can't? Well, if not, then, ladies, I think I shall finish my work and take a little nap before the dance. I love sleep more than anything else in this world."

"Have you ever stood in the girls' line at one of these

stupid dances and wanted to chop your head off and everyone else's too?" Frances said flatly to the dancer, as the mother cried, "Frances!"

"I'm not staying any longer than I have to," she told the mother, "and if you don't believe me, watch. I'm going to Nancy's and I'll stay with her for days to help her wash the car after she buys the Dutch oven, and I couldn't be happier about it! I'm not even going to tell you the rest."

Frances breathed in light sips as she spoke, afraid to inhale too much fog, afraid of the sensation that she was not really in the cabin, but instead flying, as would atoms, to all distances above and below.

"Dutch oven?" The mother sounded pleased.

"I am going further from this place than you can imagine, Linda Del-Adam," she whispered to the dancer.

"Who's Nancy?" the mother asked.

"You're a brute of a girl!" the dancer fumed, and bounded away in long, toe-pointed strides, her pale shoe-tips flinging bits of mud.

"What's the matter with you?" the mother whispered. "Can't you control yourself in front of Florida's most famous dancer? You are going to kill me, Frances. Besides, no one wants to hear your ridiculous thoughts about anything." Suddenly the mother smiled with enchantment. "Oh, did you see how that pretty little dancer came right up to us? She has the air of another world, hasn't she?"

"Stop it!" Frances hissed.

The mother glanced lingeringly across the clearing in the direction of the performer's dressing cabin. Then, hurrying to the rear of the room, she fetched a cape made of a curly type of black fur and bordered with orange and white fringe. "Frances, no more stalling. Time to head to the Hutchinson Dance Pavilion, no exceptions!"

She had a sensation akin to a rope yanking taut against a pole. "Mother—wait."

"Wait? There's no time."

"But I—I must go to Mal's dressing shack! Please!" She rang the keys in her fingers.

Bounding from the cabin, arms and legs flying, she pointed herself down the slope toward the shack near the gravel path that wound around the Hutchinson Pavilion.

"Tread upon rocks, dear, not mud!" her mother called from behind.

A shingle in the front bore Mal's name. Sensing Ray, Kenny, and the mother following, Frances fell against the shack's low-hanging eaves that gleamed humidly in the near-dusk, digging the key in the knob. She swung herself into the stale room, mud curled around her shoes. The organ's rhythmic swells were louder here, vibrating the shack's walls, ceiling, and all the surrounding shrubs and plants, each of which were surely important, but which Frances could not face or name without wishing to cry.

For how long would Frances Johnson go in circles?

By the end of the night, Frances thought, standing in the center of the shack, the mud around the pavilion would be clingier, stickier than ever, after all the towns-folk had trudged across, churning it. The mud's quality had changed over time, she noted. Years ago, after Martin French had left Munson in the heart of winter and Frances had wept dully, riding her bicycle around town, she found herself upon this same patch of mud near the pavilion, with the forest slope looming above. As she rode, she looked downward to see that her churning legs, along with the bicycle's pedals, wheels, and stem, all had been splashed with ribbons of mud so pink and runny it resembled wall-paint.

On another day, years before that, searching for a sick-bed herb with her mother and aunt, Frances had noticed a different mud patch near Munson's bakery. Its color had been a bright, speckled, alive-looking green, and a Little-Munson man stood in the middle of it. The sandy-haired, bare-chested man looked a bit wild, and was in a panic about something. He wore blue jeans. "This is it!" he shouted repeatedly, trying to hop and jerk out of the mud that nearly reached his thighs and pulled at him, and Frances' aunt grew angry. The mud spread quickly up the man's bare torso in two columns, as if eager to subsume him. No one could explain his behavior, but Frances' mother decided he was in the midst of breaking down because he had never had a good life, and so had gone wandering mindlessly into some sucking mud. It was either that, the mother said, or else the entire situation was a fluke. The man from Little-Munson wept, yelling that the mud would be as good a place as any to die.

"Quiet!" the aunt commanded him, saying she was disgusted with his dramatic display and that he was an unruly mess besides; flinging her cigarette down, turning her shoe on it, she said she would much rather sit at home with sugary coffee than look at him, and was planning to go do just that. The man fell forward on his stomach, and was able in this way to loosen himself from the bright green mud that grabbed at his body parts and pants. "It's not my fault!" he said, crawling to the edge of the mud, lying there.

"Oh, whose fault is it, then?" the aunt asked mockingly. "You're pathetic, anyone can see that, and no one's going to help you but yourself. No one wants to." Naked, the man ran away.

Frances did not care for the memory. She liked better to recall the era of the pink mud, which seemed to connote a sweeter period in her life, when she had the blank pleasures of solitude, and had lived, it seemed, with an enormous bank of time surrounding her from which each day subtracted almost nothing. Atop her wandering bicycle, gazing to the pink legs and the curious, thick time all around her, she felt a sensation of tenuous safety.

In the center of the musty shack, looking down through a jagged hole in its floor, she was aware that dozens of quiet folks, dressed up and excited, were streaming past the open door, en route to the pavilion.

Then her mother, Ray, and Kenny appeared at the shack door, the low sun behind them.

"It's not crowded yet on the dance floor," Ray observed aloud, "for the simple reason that folks find it uncomfortable to walk there, at least initially. The floor is too darned slick! They always stand at the sidelines . . . Maybe no one will dance tonight after all."

"Oh, they'll dance, all right," the mother said.

"You don't know anything about that floor, Ray," said Kenny. "It's shiny, yes, but actually not slick. The wood is special; don't you know the story of the hard trees that floated to Munson from across the sea so long ago?"

"Of course! But it's not the wood that bothers folks, Kenny. The fact is, they're all shy."

"Then why didn't you say so? You said it was because of the slick wood!"

"I did not."

"Yes, you did!" Kenny cried. "But that's wrong too.

The truth is, folks wait a long time before stepping on the dance floor in order to show respect for the wood."

"Oh, Kenny, only the very old folks do that, not the dance-goers of today!" Ray told him.

Frances did not care to listen to this quarrel. She stared through the shack doorway to the pavilion gate, squeezing her thumbs with her fingers.

"Do you know that, early this morning," the mother told them all, "I saw a baby hawk?"

Rushing, clicking fog-sensations enwrapped Frances. She looked to the gravel path, the gateway, and the pavilion itself, a large, raised, fenced-in platform lit blindingly from below and above by vaporish lights. Now the organ blew great whistling notes; these accumulated, tremblingly, before fleeing across the music's background rhythm like a train, a warning, a pattern to follow. "Mother, there's no such thing as magic, is there?" she called blankly from the doorway, lost.

Smiling, happy, light on her feet, the mother whirled on the gravel path. "How should I know? Oh, what is magic—hats and scarves? A balloon or two, little pigeons scrabbling in the dirt? There's magic in a new set of china, I know that."

Frances stepped out of the dressing shack; she wiped her brow in the fog. A sour taste sprang to her upper lip. In her hand she clenched a few cotton balls, and she grew aware, walking haltingly alongside the others, that she was jabbering. "I really don't believe in real magic . . . Mightn't what's called 'magic' actually be a kind of trickery that pretends to be artful, but is really the vulgar joke of an entrepreneur, and a very low joke at that? Do you agree? Mother, Ray—magic isn't real."

"Of course it isn't!" The mother smiled, amused.

"But, doesn't it falsely pretend to be real?" Frances felt she was losing helplessly at some obscure game of wits. "Shouldn't we say that magic is a fraud, and challenge the illusionists? Nothing can really disappear from the world, Mother, though I wish some things would."

"Shut up," the mother said sharply. "Who knows about these things, Frances?" She swooped away on the gravel path, toting a small sack of black ankle-boots, arching an arm to dance with herself, beckoning, leading the three of them closer to the pavilion gateway amidst the other party-goers. "Don't bother me about illusion now. We are busy here, because we have your life to make."

"Make, Mother?"

"We are going to get you situated. Today I simply do not want to hear about sad stories, failures, mistakes, lives gone wrong, or anything challenging or negative—not today, because I cannot control myself when I hear those horrible things. No, today, dear, we are going to make your life as happy as Linda Del-Adam's. Because if we don't, why, all the hurt and misery in the world could swim inside our door in an instant and take us like hot seawater. It will be hard work, but afterwards, our lives will be much better. Everyone in town—your father— wants you to have a better life, Frances.

"Why, I know a woman my age who left Florida for— not another state, but another country—and what did she do there? Dreamed every night of her own front porch. In that foreign place, she ate some noodles that made her sick as hell for three long years. Distant lands are filthy! Well, so is our own, but at least we know where our dirt is. I can't stomach the dirt of other nations! Neither can you, Frances." The mother smiled warmly, extending an open palm to Ray, Kenny, and then Frances, offering crackers and smaller nuts.

Eyes blazing hopefully, the mother now stood at the pavilion gateway beside the lines and groupings of quiet, dark-suited dance-goers; some peered through the gate and onto the dance floor; others faced the rock wall. Their still, sharp faces frightened Frances, and she was rooted to the path.

The gateway and its nearby walls were decorated with several colored strings. "Mother," she cried ahead to the small woman, "it's so crowded! Can't we go back to the dressing shack?"

"No!" The mother's voice was cold, cheerful.

"I want to be on my own porch," she called hopelessly, "just like the woman who ate noodles."

The mother rolled her eyes upward before plowing them drastically into Frances', moving close. "Do you expect to get every damn thing you want in this world, Frances? —Well, that's not going to happen! Will you please keep quiet?"

The organ's heaving, rocking notes blasted into the early dusk air alongside other sounds like small whistles, attenuated horns, folks' splintered voices whispering fragments of instruction, two-word questions about the bathroom, brief vows, and something like a kazoo. The sounds together formed a blare that was, she realized, indistinguishable from the organ's music itself, and Frances shuddered, unable to know what the music was, or which member of the town council was playing the enormous instrument at the head of the dance floor. She did not want to know. The busy music seemed to draw upon her heart, pulling tears forward.

She looked back toward the path and saw a queerly tilted dressing shack she had never noticed before; inside, Mrs. Mars leaned in the doorway in woolen pants, smoking, pacing, grimacing, uncharacteristically sour. Warm lamplight pooled beside her, and Frances glimpsed a tattered sofa inside the shack, bearing the weight of several legs also in pants: the four twins.

She heard someone standing at the entranceway ask, "Did Guy Jen's sister make it—?"

Another voice answered. "Nope."

"Fell off the banister," said someone else.

"Her pet housebird died th' week before!" said the first voice.

Frances lifted and dropped her shoulders repeatedly: there was nothing to do but watch, wait. She grasped for the power again, but could not find it. She hung near Ray, Kenny, and the mother, swaying as if suspended in an oily liquid, numbness inside her dark, damp shoes, thoughts recircling to the winter after Josh White disappeared, when there had been a watery, open scent across the sky, for that year there also had been a flood.

She ran quickly to Ray, bunching the fabric of his sleeve in her hand. "Listen to me," she whispered at his neck. "What is the word for a siege that occurs very fast and in silence, without anyone knowing what is happening? Oh, I can't think of it. What is that word?"

"You look good in navy blue, Frances," said Kenny.

"Do you mean 'surprise'?" Ray said.

"I don't know . . ." She looked away.

"Hello there!" Frances' mother greeted another mother at the gate. "We find this year's dance just lovely thus far." The gray-haired other mother carried no purse and wore a thin shift; she squeezed a handful of green leaves nervously, hurrying away.

"She's in trouble, actually, that mother," said Frances' mother. "She pretends to be busy, but I know the truth. She doesn't want to answer any questions about her awful adult children. Why, she makes me feel lucky—you can just look at her and see that her children's lives have made her sick. Their lives have ruined her life."

"Look!" Ray shrieked with the frightened enthusiasm of a boy, startling them all. He pointed to a cramped, dusty staircase in the wall beside the gateway, which seemed to lead to a cellar or basement. "That little door! I remember it! My father showed it to me when I was a boy—it leads to an area below the dance floor, I'm almost sure of it. It's like a secret room." He beckoned Frances, Kenny, and the mother.

"A space beneath the dance floor, like a rathskeller? But why, Ray?" It made little sense to Frances.

His brow furrowed. "Not sure. I say we go look, just for fun. My father took me down there once . . . It's always an adventure to go underneath a floor, isn't it? If I remember correctly, the ceiling is transparent. You can look overhead and see right through the dance floor above!"

"I'll go," Kenny agreed.

"Is there a waterfall?" Frances asked nervously, and the others laughed. "Yes, let's go there, please! Can't we, everyone?"

Smiling, eyes glowing, the mother spun around. "A little room beneath the Hutchinson dance floor? What a very nice idea! Is it a beautiful place? Oh, I hope so!"

The stiff door gave way under Ray's purplish fingers.

Descending a curving interior staircase, the four passed into a tile tunnel with a very low ceiling, such that they crawled through in a single line, with the mother first, Frances last, and the men in between. Then they entered a wide, echoing cellar room full of brilliant green light and vibrating with the organ's jumpy pulsations from above. The room's ceiling was low enough to bar standing comfortably upright, and the party lay down quietly to stare up through the ceiling into the room above, rich green light swarming over their faces, the room's corners jumbled with shadows, aglow.

"The ceiling's not transparent at all." Ray frowned. "It's frosted. Darn."

"The dance floor was built before any of you were born," said the mother.

"You can see the shapes of their bodies." Kenny reached excitedly, as if to touch the figures above the ceiling. "Look, folks are walking onto the dance floor right above us!"

The mother adjusted a disclike earring. "That's because they're beginning to mingle and have a marvelous time."

The cellar's echo of organ notes widened their voices, slurring and stretching sounds, making words difficult to track.

"This ceiling is costly and strong, you know," Ray observed, "because it's also a floor."

"Their faces aren't visible, but look, you can make out some details. I see a hand! It's so pretty!" Kenny's voice trembled.

"Calm down," Ray said.

Minutes passed as they watched the dark, blobbish figures above shift, meld, and separate with the rhythms of the organ music. "It is strange," Kenny went on. "Like being under the sea."

Frances turned to Ray, rolling, whispering: "What is a dance, anyhow? Lots of expectations and excitement, yes, but what else? What is it really for? I can't think, Ray."

"The people of today seek happiness and avoid pain— I guess that's about it," Ray said softly, evenly, close to her ear.

"What about soldiers? They don't seek to avoid pain."

"Sure they do."

The room indeed was like a viewing-station into an ocean, she thought, gazing upward again, detecting, she noticed, a scent of water, and she thought of terns and the tiny, unnamed, speckish creatures that floated in giant waves and quivered.

She sensed movement at her side.

"Palmer! How did you get here!?"

The physician was lying face-up beside them, his pale smile awash in the delicate green light.

"I simply followed," the man said, glancing up to the ceiling. "I'm a bit of a follower, Frances, you know. The whole town is empty now. It's kind of odd! Everyone's at the dance."

"They have to be," the mother explained.

"Such rich music!" Palmer cried, turning his head aside in pleasure, gaze soft.

"Hellooo!" Kenny called, trying to capture the attention of the dancers above, waving.

Palmer turned to his side. "You were right, Frances,

you son of a gun. Munson folks have their dances after all."

Her eyes glistened toward him. "Palmer . . . are you angry?"

"About—?"

"The oil."

"Ah. Frances, no. I'll procure the oil another way, and continue working on the balm on my own. Don't worry. You must find your own course! But aren't you—?"

"What?"

"—Afraid to face Carol?"

Sweat jumped to her lip. "I'm not. Beginning today and from now on, I won't be afraid."

Palmer's wheaty-colored eyes were close, and with his slipping glasses and the large, wagging hand passing beneath his hip as he tried to shift positions, he seemed the funniest person she had ever known; her heart slid, as if in liquid. "I can't bear to look at Carol today or any day," the man panted, twisting. "That would remind me of myself long ago."

"Are you two gossiping?" It was Kenny.

The thunderous organ began anew, and the mother giggled. "Everyone, look at all the pretty lights and the folks swaying with the music! It's just lush."

"I'll have to admit she's right," said Ray, his teeth a luminous green.

Frances mumbled quietly to Palmer, "After a few moments at the dance, I will leave, without a word. I'll help Nancy with her cooking, the car, and the raisin, after all. I don't know why I should feel so close to her when I see her so rarely, but—"

"I wouldn't think about a raisin right now," Palmer

advised.

"It's lovely," said the mother, "but it is also stuffy in here."

"I'll talk to Nancy for a long, long time," Frances went on stolidly.

"What *do* you talk about with other girls, Frances?" Kenny asked, head turning.

"Oh, lots of things, Kenny—"

"—Dolls?"

"No!"

Folks now crowded above; then shadows of the dark-dressed party-goers moved slow and fast with the organ's chords that gashed the air, and Frances could not remember when she had not been here, beneath the blurry dance floor, watching.

She whispered minute scraps of words to herself and their sounds flew across the green cellar walls with the echoing organ notes, fading instantly as water-stains.

She raised one hand toward the ceiling, pressing the other to the floor, half-sitting, pushing with all her strength, wincing, as if this were the last thing in life for her to do.

"After helping Nancy, I'll leave for good!" she said forcefully, excited, expelling air.

"What are you two discussing, dear?" the mother called back, her face small at the end of the room.

"Nothing!" she cried.

"Does anyone know the story about long ago, when this dance pavilion site was a natural lake?" Kenny asked. "They filled it in with earth and built the pavilion when a girl drowned there."

"A girl drowned? Oh! Who was she?" Frances cried.

"Town waitress," Kenny answered. "She swam in the lake, then drowned. The lake turned her body to soap."

"Oh, no!"

"I heard about that," Ray said.

"Years later, the body floated up, and they pulled it out of the lake, but when no one was looking, they sunk it back into the water and couldn't find it again when they tried. It must be true," Kenny explained. "Town legends usually are."

"No they're not!"

"Hurry!" the mother called, moving back to the tile hallway that led to the stair. "We're all going back to the dance now!"

"Frances," Palmer whispered, scooting closer. His nose shone. "I know this day is a difficult one for you. Don't worry about the soap-legend."

"I said come along!" the mother called.

"Oh, Palmer: if I were different—a different kind of woman—I would have been able to fetch the oil for you," she whispered tearily, sweating with the tile floor cold beneath her. "And I wouldn't be here now!"

Scooting along with the others, Frances heard a strange scraping noise at a distance. Shadows whirled on her face; the organ's echoic notes floated.

"Men," she called frantically to Ray, Kenny, and Palmer, her mind jumping to and fro, "How do the battles and sieges of history get named? For example—Vicksburg—did a commander consider the name carefully before deciding on it, or did low-level soldiers just casually choose the name that best described the fight until that name spread and took hold? What if some standoffs go unnamed?"

"Battles were always named fairly quickly," Ray answered, scooting nearby. "Army commanders would call their leaders on the telephone to tell them what had happened on the field. More than one army might have reported action, and this is why some battles have two names. Yes, some battles go unnamed."

The scraping noise grew louder.

"Follow me, all!" The mother was moving up the stairs.

"But what if a siege isn't named?" Frances panted back to Ray.

"Gone. Like it never happened," Ray answered.

"But where does it go? Oh, it must be listed somewhere in Europe, in a directory, right?"

"My, the dance is picking up. Look at those shadows!" Palmer spoke admiringly, looking back to the ceiling, swaying his head in musical rhythm.

Frances could not bear the scraping sound any longer. She raised her head high. "Do you hear that? Is it upstairs on the dance floor, or down here? Ray? Mother?"

The sound persisted. Then she glanced back to a far corner of the cellar, noticing a small cabinet door at the base of the wall, green-stained with the room's light. Sprinting there, head down to avoid the ceiling, she fell upon the door's handle, knowing it would be locked. Her veins chilled when she heard a dog's bark. "Missie!" she cried. She turned to the others, who stood across the room, watching. "Men! We've got to open this cabinet—look, the door's so small! Ray! Who has the key?"

"I don't know," Ray answered, scooting toward her, head bent. "This is the type of lock they use in cities. I haven't seen any like that before. It's new—brass."

"Please open it, men! Missie's in there!" Frances half-stood, then fell to her knees before the little door.

"To find the key, you could either call the cabinet-builder or the pavilion-keeper," Kenny offered.

"We could just smash the door in," Ray said.

"No, no! Don't do that—it might hurt Missie!" In the coolness of her limbs were fathoms of dark, and her tears were sparrows melting on the floor. She tore into her dress pocket for the key-ring with the keys to Mal's buildings, her own house and Nancy, and also a small, blunt-nosed key that fit a lockable toaster case—another of her household inventions—which now seemed centuries old.

Face to the floor, Frances raised an arm high. "Men, take these keys, will you—Ray? Palmer? Anyone! Happy? Take them and melt them down, do you hear, at the Hutchinson Dance Pavilion foundry—it's not so far from here . . . Please, mold a key for this lock and bring it back to me! Oh, hurry, please, Missie's in there! Take the doorknob with you!" Handing off the key-ring, she pressed her face back to the cellar floor because it needed to be there, and her mind volleyed to a point somewhere in the distance, in the future or the past, where she corresponded precisely with herself, and where she was most alone.

One of the brothers lifted the key-ring from her hand. "Hmm, she's right. We could liquefy these pretty easily at the foundry," Ray's voice said. "It won't take long, once we get the heat going."

"Yes!" Her arms muffled her cry.

"We could add a few coins or nails to the mixture, for volume," Kenny said. "It'll be easy. Don't worry,

Frances, we'll help you." He knocked the doorknob off the cabinet with his shoe, catching it in his hand. The dog yelped.

"Missie!" she cried.

"Jes' rip th' door down with an axe, is what I say." Mal had joined them.

"No!" Frances howled to the floor. "Not an axe, Mal! Missie will die!" She squeezed her ears shut.

How would Frances Johnson learn and bear?

"Frances?" a voice said. It was Lucas.

"Oh—what are you doing down here, Lucas?" She lifted her head. "Little-Munson folks don't usually mix at our dances,"

"I wanted to," he said plainly.

"Lucas! Are you changing? You seem so different today! You're so dressed-up and polite . . . Has everything in the world changed? Look, there's no cotton in your ears. That's good! Don't you—"

"I'm not using the cotton lately."

"Why not, Lucas?"

"I have a thousand ways to protect myself," he said with a little tune.

"Ah—then—Lucas, can you help me?" she cried, hiding her face again. "Missie's in there!" she flailed a finger. Bending near, Lucas waited a long moment, then held her wrist to stay its trembling.

Then she heard the sounds of other folks squeezing into the cellar doorway, talking, gathering, noting the room, its light, and its low ceiling, while Frances remained crouched by the cabinet door.

"A dog? I doubt a dog could thrive in that little place," said Mrs. Mars.

"Dogs have always enjoyed small, private spaces throughout the centuries." It was Heidi, diminutive, stooped, gripping a cane.

"Hidden grass dens are best for dogs. I saw it in a picture book," said Ray Mars.

"Frances? I tried to call you." It was Curly-Dawn, Kenny's girlfriend, pulling at Frances' arm, her eyes shadowed by dark rings. "I got so sick!" The girl trembled such that the material of her new, stiff dress nearly rattled. "I thought you might know of a cure, since you know the doctor so well."

"Curly, you don't look good! Why are you at the dance when you should be resting in bed?"

"I had to come, Frances! I can't be alone. But it's fine—I can rest here at the dance, in a chair."

"Please, please, everyone—let's calm down and go upstairs to the dance where we belong!" the mother still called out from a distance.

Frances' answer came equally stubbornly, bellowing across the room. "Not now, mother!"

How was Frances Johnson both small and large?

"Odd, 'ent it, dog in th' wall." Mal coughed.

Other voices spread through the cellar.

"Dil Spreen was missin' a few months all told, did y' know?"

"He turned up?" The voice was Ming's.

"Barely. He went crazy, then died of it."

"I knew it."

"Same thing'll happen to young Mary, you'll see."

A woman's voice shouted to everyone: "Come on back, you spoilsports!" Frances peered out from her hands. The beckoning woman was stout, resembling, around the eyes, Linda Del-Adam. "Head upstairs to the gate; you won't know what's good 'til you do. There's crackers with cheese, an' I put lettuce on top—for moisture!"

Folks began filtering back upstairs, though Frances remained, head down, sunk, unable to imagine moving. She would not leave Munson now; she would not go anywhere, because she belonged here in the cellar beside Missie, which had always been true and she had not seen it. The floor adjoined her body; so did Munson, her family, townsfolk—and little else, for these were the real things, Frances knew, breathing in relief. The fog in her lungs was not the worst thing, she discovered.

When can people surpass themselves best?

She called into her hands with a braying sound commensurate with all buried wishes.

"When I want to speak to Nancy, I really cannot wait!" she hollered, uncertain if anyone was there to hear. The gleaming blue seam into which Nancy would someday slip away for good hovered in her mind, darkness licking it above and below.

"Oh, hurry, brothers, cast the key! . . . I only want to open the door, get her out; just hurry, oh, who, who, would put Missie in a place like that, and why?" But she knew.

"I can't say I didn't, Frances, but please don't misunderstand," said a burnished voice.

"Oh—Doctor Carol!"

Mark Carol moved close, sitting beside her in an awkward position, bending his own head softly and kissing Frances with a soft, large, fleshy movement undulating like waves of salt-water.

I'll be what you make me.

It was everything.

How far would Frances Johnson go?

His lips seemed wider than a face to Frances, and from within the kiss she found astonishment, repulsion, and a plopping noise like the sound of a frog landing in a swamp, a sound that infuriated her. The doctor ceased kissing and waited, his face near.

Where was the terminus for Frances Johnson?

With the slyness of one seeking to bring ignominy to a mate, she stole her hand inside his lab-coat pocket, feeling a small notebook, a shoe-horn, and, presently, an apple, which she pulled from the pocket, its stem enmeshed by dark hair. She derived a sour enjoyment from holding Mark Carol's arm as he pulled her up, and the two strolled around the perimeter of the room, heads bent low. Frances enjoyed the man's arm, which was stronger than Ray's. The plopping noise still rang in her ears.

"Is there a frog?" She looked behind.

The doctor regarded her. "Frances, listen to me: as a rule, I notice nice things. You, for instance. I knew you were nice."

"What does 'nice' mean?" Their voices echoed in the cellar.

"It means you are good."

"What did you do with my dog?"

"Ah, no—nothing. I simply found the dog, saw its tag, and all quite accidentally! Please: I meant well. Don't worry about your pet. It's being kept in a safe place for now, and later tonight, my secretary will take care of everything and return it home. I knew you would be here; that's why I came. How old are you, Frances?"

"... I'm ..."

"It can't be possible."

"What?"

"You. I've never known a girl like you. You're grand—
and I'm not talking silly, Frances. You don't flutter your
eyes or swing your hips as you walk, do you? You're different than the others. You know, I think we're going to
have a fine summer, one we'll be stronger for in the fall."

"Can you be real?" Frances discovered she was extraordinarily shy.

"Real enough to take you my prisoner," he teased,
smiling, breathing her hair.

Could Frances Johnson be strong enough?

The sounds of the dance still thrummed above, and as
she gazed upward through the ceiling, the form of Linda
Del-Adam hovered over her, the diaphanous skirt shivering, shifting. The dancer's face bent down to the floor,
the big, dark, blurry eyes peering through the glass for
a moment before she flew away. Frances and the doctor
walked, and she noted that the fog had receded almost
completely, or else had become part of the atmosphere.
She closed her eyes, not caring where she was or why.

"By the way, are *you* real? Ha!" said Doctor Carol.

"Ray won't like this," she said sadly.

Where could Frances Johnson go?

"Not everyone gets just exactly what he wants, you
know," the new doctor informed her. "But Ray will find
contentment someday, I'm sure."

She said, "Did you know that Missie was a very stubborn pet? She never wanted to give in."

He smiled with calm blue eyes.

"Missie was content for a long, long time, but she
never took the easy road. Once, out of stubbornness,

she stayed outside almost a week without food, and very nearly crumbled! She got better, though. Quiet as she was, Missie was too resentful—for a dog. She couldn't manage to stay with me, in the end. She left!"

Now heat expanded Frances' body easily, sensually, and she did not need to try at all. Mark Carol pulled her lightly to him; again they walked around the cellar. His dry hand was not bad, Frances thought, smiling in response to his large smile.

Had Frances Johnson finished or begun?

She heard steps.

What is a trap; what is not?

Ray entered the doorway alone, hair windblown, stripping a fresh stick.

"Ray!" she called across to him. "Listen," she said as he approached with footsteps clicking in the empty room, "Is life sad?"

Ray thought. "I suppose it is—or part of it is, yes."

"Be honest!"

"That is honest."

"So it's a fact?"

"Oh, Frances."

"Why is it true?"

"Hmmm." Ray stared toward the dim corner. He dug a hand in his pocket.

"Certain aspects of life are undoubtedly sad, yes, I'll wager," Doctor Carol interjected as the three began to stroll together.

She snorted. "Well, Ray?"

He looked exasperated, glancing at the doctor. "Frances, that question is—well, I don't think it's the best question. It's not very focused or exact."

"But if it were the question?" She was hot behind the eyes.

"Well, no one around here likes to be very close or comfortable together, whether it's on a path, in a little shop, or under any circumstances whatsoever," he said at last, awkwardly. "We made the key, Frances," he added.

"That's all right, Ray," she said.

She took his arm, while Doctor Carol continued to hold her other arm, and they all walked. "I didn't need to make a decision about today at all, Ray," she whispered. "Did you see what happened? The decision made itself."

"You let go, Frances."

"Oh. Letting go is wrong?"

"No, Frances, no. Everyone does that. That's how the future comes."

What is possible; what is not?

＊　　＊　　＊

Hours later, long after nightfall, the three of them—Frances, Ray, and Doctor Carol—lay quietly in the clearing outside the darkened dance pavilion on cool, bare ground, having climbed from the cellar at the dance's end.

The doctor was asleep, snoring; Frances lay beside Ray in the soft, fogless air. The organ's whistles resounded in her mind though they were long finished, and the day's end brought damp, swirling relief.

Was Frances Johnson similar to others?

"But I didn't accomplish a thing," she fretted, near sleep, then separate from it, tossing. "I didn't make a decision. I did nothing."

Ray turned stiffly on his side. "The dance is generally

always a draining event, Frances."

What kind of pattern brings no relief?

"I didn't leave. How could I have done things differently?" she asked, burdened.

"You know, Frances," Ray remarked, lying there, "I was thinking recently about the Red Baron. He originally wanted to paint his plane red, but the other pilots told him no. 'That will make you a target,' they said. But after some time, they all painted their planes red too, and flew them everywhere—maybe because the Baron was so charming and powerful. Those pilots just couldn't help painting their planes. Frances, maybe you are like those men. You just couldn't help coming to the dance. You couldn't resist it."

"Oh, Ray. I'll bet that story isn't even true." She was drowsy again, docked in the oily night.

To which places would Frances Johnson go?

She heard the minuscule sounds of the insects' feet in the leaves beyond. She looked at him more closely. "Ray, are you blue because of all this—and Doctor Carol?" She nodded behind her, toward the doctor.

A tear loitered across his face. Above, trees in the night breathed while Ray and Frances, shiveringly cool, slept.

Running steps woke her.

"Frances!"

"I'm awake." Her tongue stuck. The sky was seethingly bright. Kenny's eyes shone eagerly, and his hair was combed with water. "Frances, will you come home?" He glanced at the snoring doctor, whose head jutted to one side. "Folks are at your house now. We put a kettle on, and everyone has changed their mind! We see now that Mark Carol isn't as good as we thought. We were wrong.

He's not right for you! Your mother said to come find you. Frances, do you think you would enjoy the floral business? Enoch Ruth mentioned it for your future. Oh, hurry home, won't you? Everything will be all right—Mal thinks so, and your father does, too."

"—What?" she faltered, blinking, pressing a palm to the earth, then dropping back to its coolness again, hearing Kenny run back through the woods the way he came.

Foliage rustled there for a moment, then her mother emerged from the same path, out of breath, a clutch of green branches in her arms.

"It's all over, dear, did you hear? Well, sometimes with hindsight, the world looks all different, isn't that strange? Let's go. Oh, don't mention Mark Carol again—gee, he turned out to be a real crumb-bum! There are others, though, Frances: you'll see. Say something, won't you dear?" asked the mother, pulling on a shoe, wandering away.

The clearing was quiet again. Frances turned, her face to Ray's shirt. "What to do now, Ray?"

"Don't know, Frances," he muttered from sleep.

9 781891 241291